MARRIED TO A BROWNSVILLE BULLY

JAHQUEL J.

A Note From The Author

Book 49! I keep recounting to make sure I didn't over count or miss anything, but this is book 49 for Jahquel J. I appreciate you all for sticking with me through everything. I came into this industry in 2014 and came right into love and support from everyone. I'm not just talking about you readers, I'm talking about all the authors who support my work and shout me out too. It's much appreciated, and I see you. Keep on pushing, Queens and Kings, we got this.

Now, about this book. I've had six storylines for this book and this is the only one that I fell in love with. Golden is hardheaded, stubborn and independent. She's also loving, caring and will give her last to help someone out. I absolutely loved writing about Golden and Gyan. Like I tell you with every book, I write based on how it comes to me. This book is what I like to call the introductions to the characters. There's so much drama, but you're still getting to know the characters as well. This series will be a two-book series, and I will be coming with book two the first week of June **Fingers crossed**

With Yoshon, he's older, mature and just wants a family. He has experienced heartbreak and that's why he's perfect for Golden. I don't know if you've noticed, but I've been making all my characters a tad bit older. If they aren't in their early thirties, they're in their late thirties. Yoshon is thirty-eight and a grown ass man, so you won't find that young back and forth ish with him. He knows what he wants and has no problem going after it.

Enough of me babbling. Here's the book and I just wanted to thank you all for supporting me and my publishing company as well. We appreciate it.

Much Love,
   Jah

www.facebook.com/JahquelJ
http://www.instagram.com/_Jahquel
http://www.twitter.com/Author_Jahquel
Be sure to join my reader's group on Facebook
www.facebook.com/ Jahquel's we reading or nah?

Yolani - YO – LA- NEE
Yoshon - YO – SHAWN

PROLOGUE

"What do you mean he's being released in two months? Ho...How could this have happened?" I panicked as the detective sat in front of me and told me life-shattering news.

"You husband has powerful connections and his lawyer has pulled some strings. They filed an appeal and my connections told me that he could be out in under two months. I felt the need to warn you because we worked so closely together during your case," the detective explained.

Her explanation didn't make any of her news better. In fact, it made my heart pound out my chest and caused me to look over my son playing so peacefully in the play area of the McDonalds we chose to meet at.

"This man has raped and beat my ass in front of our child. Then, he almost killed me, and you're telling me that he's set to be released in two months."

"Golden, I'm sorry. I'm sorry that this is happening to you. Your husband is rich and has people in high places. You couldn't have thought that he would be behind bars forever."

"Not forever. I did, however, think that the judicial system would do something to protect me and my son."

She dropped her head. I could tell that she was disappointed, but there was nothing that she could do about it. "I suggest you get out of town, Golden. Take you and Gyan and move away and start a new life."

"Start a new life? With what money? He has blocked me from everything. I've been trying to make ends meet with the little bit of savings that I do have."

Reaching into her pocket, she peeled off a couple hundred dollars. "Take it and get it out of town. Virginia isn't safe for you anymore.

"With seven hundred dollars? The three hundred dollars you gave me and the four hundred I have left in the hotel?"

"My hands are tied, Golden. I wasn't supposed to tell you this bit of information just yet. I thought you should know so you can get yourself and your son out of town." She stood up, embraced me and then headed out the restaurant.

I sat there with the weight of my world on my shoulders. A year ago, I had a home, car and anything my heart desired. My son was in one of the best private schools, and all I did was shop. My husband, Grand, made sure I got every and anything I wanted. Money wasn't an object and I ate it all up. After all, I've been with him since I turned eighteen. He was my first in everything and you couldn't tell me that I wasn't making the best decision of my life. I left New York City, and left my grandmother behind. She disapproved of Grand, and if I would have known then what I know now, I would have listened to her. She told me he was trouble and that I shouldn't get involved with him, but when you're young, you're dumb as shit. At that time, I was eighteen with a man handing me large amounts of money, clothes and anything else I wanted. All I had to do was snap my fingers, and he would make it happen.

At twenty, I had our son Gyan, and my entire world changed. I had a little baby looking into my eyes that depended on me. When I brought him to New York to visit my grandmother, she begged for me to leave. I mean, I did show up to her house wearing a pair of thick Chloe glasses that hid a black eye. Not even two weeks after my son was born, Grand put his hands on me for falling asleep before fixing our son a bottle. Right then and there, I should have removed myself and my son, but I didn't. After each hit, an apology came and eventually an engagement ring came, then a wedding ring. I married this stupid son of a bitch and the abuse stopped. My grandmother cut me out of her life and I hadn't spoken to her since that day she called me a 'damn dummy.' The day before our wedding I made him promise that he wouldn't put his hands on me anymore. For what it's worth, he hadn't hit me for a full four years.

For my twenty-fifth birthday, he sent me away on vacation with my girlfriends. The night before, I felt bad being away from my husband on my day. I decided to surprise him and come home early. Imagine my surprise when I walk into our home and he's laid up with a chick in our theater room watching a movie. The woman had on my pajama set and she had a baby in a bassinet beside them. How would you react? I reacted like every woman in America would have. I beat the living shit out the woman and hauled off and slapped my husband. Grand knew I was serious when I took our son and stayed at a hotel suite. I had no other family and the friends I did have I made through Grand. All my girlfriends were his friend's wives, so where could I go? They weren't about to stand up to the men that financed their lives, so I took my son and checked into a hotel.

After about a week, Grand blocked our credit cards. Still, I used the cash to stay another week until I had no choice but to head home and talk about what went down. Not only did Grand have an affair on me, but he had a daughter with the bitch. He told me how I was going to learn my place and to start respecting his child's mother. He said this while yelling and pointing his hands in my face while our son watched. When he had enough of my mouth, he knocked me in the mouth and continued to beat the shit out of me while our son cried and tried to fight him off me. After he put our son in his bedroom and locked the door, he dragged me to our bedroom and continued to beat the shit out of me until it aroused him. That's when he raped me in the middle of our white fur rug. I had never been so violated in my life. Having the man who was supposed to love and cherish you, violate you right there in the room that was supposed to be sacred for the both of you.

When he was done, he pulled his pants up, spit on me and told me to fix myself and to feed his son. Soon as he left out the door, I grabbed my son and went to the police station and pressed charges on him. I went through everything to make sure he didn't see the day of light. When he was sentenced to five years, it was the happiest day of my life. Now, six months later and he was getting out because he knew people in high places. Now, I had to figure out how I was going to survive off seven hundred dollars with a child? My phone deterred me from my thoughts as it rang loudly in the pockets of the sweats I wore.

"Hey," I answered.

"What did she say?" Grand's sister was the only person that didn't agree with what her brother did.

"Your brother found a way to get out way earlier than his sentence. She couldn't tell me much except get out of town."

"Get out of town? Golden, what are you going to do? You can't stay in Virginia." Teri panicked.

"Teri, I feel like giving up," I sobbed and put my head in my hand. My son was five and was smart. He wasn't a dumb child and it was because life had caused him to grow up quickly. These six months he had to grow up more than ever.

"Listen, you need to go to New York until you can figure out what to do. New York is too big for him to find you there. Last he was saying; he was moving Tamika into the house with their daughter. I'm going to have Sam get you a bucket from his dealership and I'll give you some cash to last you."

"I appreciate you so much, Teri."

"Bring Gyan over here so I can see him. I know I'm not going to see you guys for a while," she told me and I sighed.

Teri always had my back. She knew living with her brother was the devil and had no problem speaking on when he was wrong. Unlike the rest of their family, Teri didn't live off her brother's money. Her husband owned a string of dealerships throughout Richmond, Virginia. Grand's mama always took his side because he paid for her life. Not Teri, she hated how he treated me and how he cheated on me. There were rumors that he cheated on me, but I never paid them any mind. Apparently, Grand was cheating on me and had a few children too.

"I will," I promised.

If I knew Grand, he wasn't going to wait two months. He was going to push his lawyers to get him out sooner, so I needed to move quickly. Grabbing Gyan, I quickly got into a cab and headed to our motel.

"Mommy, where are we going?" he questioned as I packed all our things into our bags. I made sure I didn't leave anything behind.

"We're going on a little trip. It'll be fun," I offered him a weak smile.

"I'll follow you anywhere, Mommy." He smiled and caused my heart to skip a beat. Gyan was truly my heart and I loved him with all of me.

"You have no choice, kid," I winked.

After I packed all our things, Teri was downstairs waiting for us. She told me not to bother coming to her house, and she would meet us at the motel. When I got downstairs with Gyan, she had a 2004 Nissan Maxima waiting.

"What's this?"

"This is your new car. Sam has it registered in his sister's name, so you're good."

Tears fell down my cheeks as I looked at Teri. "You know I'm going to miss you, right?"

"I'm going to miss you too, babe. Especially my nephew, but when the time is right, we'll see each other. Just keep me posted with a quick message, so I know you're alright."

"I will..." my voice trailed off.

"Gold, you're doing this for your son. He's what you need to be focused on. Grand is poison, and Gyan doesn't need to see that." She pulled me into a tight hug. "When are you planning on leaving?"

Taking a deep breath, I looked up at our motel room. "Tonight."

"Tonight? Why so soon?"

"Your brother is going to push to be released sooner. He's not a man with much patience."

"And this is why he should of married you and done right by you. You've always had his best interest at heart." She bent down and kissed Gyan. "I love you, baby boy and don't you forget that."

"I love you too, Auntie." He kissed her back.

Standing up, she stared at me as she wiped tears from her eyes. "Here's some money. Please text me an emoji from whatever new phone you get. I'll know it's you."

"I'll be sure to send you an eggplant emoji," I tried to lighten the mood.

"Only you, Golden. I'm gonna miss you, my sweet sister." She hugged me once more. Her Uber pulled into the parking lot and she handed me over the keys. "I love you both," she sniffled.

"Love you too, Teri. This isn't goodbye," I told her. If it was in God's plans, we will cross paths again.

Teri watched us through the window as the car pulled out of the parking lot. Taking Gyan's hand, we headed back to our room to continue packing. Gyan took a bath and I showered then we changed into some comfy clothes before we checked out and got on the road. Before getting on the road, we stopped at CVS and grabbed some snacks for the road, then hit the road.

"Baby boy, new beginnings."

"New Beginnings, Mom." He smiled as we pulled out the CVS parking lot and got on the road. Richmond, Virginia had been my home since I was eighteen, and now I was heading back to where I truly belonged; New York City.

1

Golden

Six Months later....

"I'M SORRY! I'M SORRY!" I yelled as I rushed into Gyan's classroom. It was parent-teacher conference and I was over an hour late.

"It's fine, Ms. Stewarts," she smiled. "Gyan told me that you work at Starbucks and white people love their coffee," his teacher repeated, and I couldn't hide my embarrassment.

"Gyan, stop repeating everything you hear," I scolded him slightly and sat down at her desk. "How's he doing?"

"Gyan is a pleasure to have. We love having him in our school and he's so smart to be six years old."

"Thank you. On my time off, I try to tutor him and make sure he knows his stuff. He's always been a happy and smart child."

"I can see. This meeting is short and sweet, just keep doing whatever you're doing. As his teacher, I appreciate it." She smiled as I shook her hand. She was a young, black woman with short natural hair.

"No, thank you. I'm sorry again for being late. It won't happen at the next conference," I assured her as I grabbed Gyan's backpack and we headed out of her classroom.

As we walked out of the school's building, I smiled. My son had witnessed so much and he still managed to be a rock star in school. Nothing seemed to surprise me with him anymore.

"You're awesome." I smiled.

"I know," he laughed.

"Guess what?" I asked when we got closer to the car.

"What?"

"I got you some new sneakers," I popped the trunk and showed him the Nike box. "You thought I forgot all about your birthday gift, huh?"

"Mommy, you didn't have to," he told me, which made me feel worse.

Since moving to New York, it hadn't been easy. I went crawling back to my grandmother, only to find out she died two years prior. It hit me like a ton of bricks that the only family I had was now six feet under. Grand put so much in my head about my grandmother that after she cut me off, I didn't bother to call or keep in contact. After the shock of that hit me, I had to find us somewhere to live. How could I do that when I barely had money? We stayed in hotels for the first few months but then money dried up. I had to get a job at Starbucks and enroll Gyan in school. For his birthday last month, I couldn't afford to buy him what I wanted to. Instead, I got him an action figure off the clearance rack at target. As a mother, my heart was crushed hearing my son tell me what I didn't have to do, all because he knew money was tight.

"Gyan, don't tell me what I don't have to do. I want you to have them, so you can look fresh," I smiled.

"Thanks, Mommy. I love them." He hugged me tightly.

"You're welcome, baby."

As we piled into the car, he moved his Superman comforter and pillow over and buckled himself in. I hated that we slept in our car, but that was all I could afford. A studio apartment in New York was over a thousand dollars, and the shelters were all over-crowded. I refused to put my baby in the shelter. Our car wasn't perfect, but it was home to us. It kept us warm and safe from being robbed in the homeless shelter. I was going to make a way to get us a roof over our head. I worked every shift that was offered to me and didn't turn none down. When Gyan was with me, he would sit in the corner seat with his books while I worked. He understood that I needed the hours and the money for us to live. One thing I prided my baby on was never going to bed hungry. He went to bed with a full stomach and we went to my job right before school, so he could wash up.

Like the detective said, Grand was released early on proba-tion. He couldn't leave the state and had a bunch of limitations. Soon as I crossed over into Delaware, I tossed my phone out the window while driving on the bridge. All I had now was a cheap android phone that I used to keep in contact with Teri. She called once a week and updated me on things. Teri thought we had an apartment, I worked a good job, and Gyan was in private school. I lied and told her all those things because I didn't want her feeling like she had to send me money. She and Sam had kids of their own and mouths to feed. I laid down and had my son, so I needed to be grown enough to provide for him. Every morning and every night, I continued to tell myself that it wasn't for forever. I would be up on my luck and wouldn't have to live like this. Grabbing my ringing cell, I saw my co-worker's number flash across the screen.

"What's up, Cindy?"

"Can you work for me tonight? I have cramps and I'm tired," she whined in the phone. Cindy was some Spanish girl that always called out. I worked at Starbucks by the day and stocked shelves at Target at night. She was actually the one person I could call a friend. Plenty of nights she offered her couch to me and Gyan but I turned it down.

"Sure."

"Thanks. Bring Gyan over so he can have a warm meal and bed tonight," she demanded. "My shift is overnight, so come and rest until your shift."

"We'r—"

"Golden, this wasn't a request. More like a demand," she told me and ended the call. Cranking the car up, I pulled out of the school's parking lot and headed to Cindy's apartment.

Cindy lived in the hood and she wasn't afraid to let you know. I didn't care if she lived in the devil's den, long as my son had somewhere safe to sleep that was all that mattered to me. I pulled onto her block and found a parking spot by the grace of God. Grabbing my purse and overnight bag for both Gyan and myself, we walked through the projects until we came across her building. Taking the pissy elevator up, we got off, and Cindy had the door opened and waiting for us.

"Get in here," she pulled us inside her apartment. "These crackheads were just arguing out there not too long ago," she explained as she locked the door.

"Aren't they always bickering back and forth?"

"Yeah, but I heard her scream and ain't heard her since. Anyway, Gyan you know the drill. Go take your hour bath you love so much, and I'll have some nuggets and corn on the table for you."

"I appreciate you, Cindy."

"No, I appreciate you. You sit down and relax until work later on. I know you need the hours, so grab them up."

"I can't wait until things look up. I'm thinking of moving down south if it doesn't look up soon."

"Back down south?"

"In Georgia," I revealed.

Opening the fridge, she pulled out two beers. "Things will look up for you, I promise," she told me.

"Hope so," I sighed as I cracked open the beer and kicked my shoes off. "What's new with you?"

"Nothing much. Darian wants to move in with me and I don't know how to feel about it," she announced.

Cindy and her long-time boyfriend had been going back and forth about living together for months. Each time I think they're going to do it, Cindy switches her mind and calls it off.

"Well, are you going to go through with it this time?"

"I actually think I am. We've been talking about it since I called it off the last time, and I think I'm ready for it."

"I'm happy for you, C. Darian makes you happy, so you should live together and make beautiful Spanish babies."

"Have a bunch of little Adobo babies running around," she joked.

"Yess!"

"How's the apartment hunt going?"

"I've seen a few and they were too expensive. I found a basement apartment in Queens. I'm just waiting for the lady to get back to me."

"Hopefully you get it. It's far from me, but I'll make the trip. Until you do, it's winter and cold. You and Gyan can stay here. It's the least I could do; you always come through for me."

Leaning up, I stared her in the eye. She had to be joking with me. If it wasn't February, I would have sworn it was April Fool's day. "Cindy, are you serious?"

"Yes. I feel bad that you both are sleeping in your car. Stay here for as long as you need and pay for what you can. Darian will be moving him soon, so it'll be tight, but we'll make it work."

I jumped up and hugged her so tight that she spilled some of her beer. "I appreciate you so much," I cried as I held her.

"Gold, you're a good mother trying to do the best you can for your child. I'll never knock that and I want to support that as much as I can."

"I'm just praying it all makes sense, you know?"

"It will, Golden. You're a good mother and it will work out for you."

"Thank you," I smiled and sipped my beer. While I had time, I was going to enjoy the TV, relax and get some food before heading back out to work. We laughed at Gyan splashing in the bathroom. He always made a mess in Cindy's bathroom and she never minded cleaning it. It was as if seeing him smile made it all worth it to her.

I DRAGGED myself out my car and through the projects to get to Cindy's building. After spending all night on my feet, all I wanted to do was lay on the couch for a good hour before I had to take Gyan to school. Working two jobs, raising my son and trying to keep my sanity was hard. Sometimes I wanted to go back to Virginia with my tail tucked between my legs. If I apologized to Grand, he would get us a condo, and we could co-parent our son together. Then, I got the urge to call his phone and tell him to suck my balls. I just prayed that Gyan didn't resent me when he got older. It wasn't like he was a baby and didn't know who his father was. He never asked about him and that worried me. Was he trying to protect my feelings? Or did he not truly give a shit about his father?

"Move on out the way, Beauty Queen," The crackhead from across the hall spat as she pushed the door open and checked the mail.

"Excuse your stink ass too... Smelling like a pound of crack and chicken," I shot back and pressed the elevator door.

"Bitch, if this check ain't in here, I'm gonna take my anger out of you."

"Listen, Ms. Crackhead Sally, you touch me, and I'm gonna whip your ass so bad that you gonna be running the crack on your bruises instead of smoking it." When she saw me place my work bag down, she backed her ass up toward the mailboxes and left me the hell alone.

If threatening crackheads early in the morning was the price I had to pay for having a warm roof over my head, then I was willing to do it every morning. When I told Gyan what Cindy told me, he was so happy and excited that he had somewhere warm to sleep until we found a place to live. I knocked on the door and waited for Cindy to answer. When she did, she was already dressed in workout attire with a cup of coffee in her hand.

"Good morning!" she smiled. "Here, take some." She handed me the cup of coffee as I placed my work bag on the floor.

"Why are you so loud?"

"Girl, I'm always loud in the morning. I took it upon myself to get Gyan ready for school. You go and get some sleep; I'll drop him off when I bring Darian to work."

"Darian?"

"Yeah, he came over last night. We talked all night and decided that we are going to move forward with moving in together. I really love this man, Golden." She poured some Captain Crunch into a bowl.

"Awe, I'm glad that you both were able to come to an agreement about y'all situation."

"Yeah, I'm glad too. For a minute I was worried about what would happen between us. I'm not ready to move on with no one and he's who I want to be with," she went on and on about her boyfriend.

"Mommy, how was work?"

"It was good, baby. How did you sleep?"

"Like an angel." He sat down as Cindy put down the cereal in front of him.

"Good. You sure you want to take him to school? I can run him there, so it doesn't take time out of your day."

"He's fine, Golden. I'll drop him first and then go drop Darian before heading to the gym. You need to be worried about getting some sleep. Don't your work at Starbucks around four?"

"Yeah," I sighed.

"Need me to pick him up from school?"

"Cindy, I don't want you to fe—"

"I'll pick him up," she cut me off. "I want to help you out, sis. It's not a problem for me to scoop him up after my hair appointment, I'm off today anyways," she further explained.

"Thank you."

"Don't mention it. Gyan, come on so you won't be late."

"This my first time not being there for free breakfast," he jumped down from the chair and went to grab his book bag. "Bye, Mommy."

"Later, babe. I love you so much." I kissed his forehead.

Darian came out the bedroom with his work clothes on. He was a Jamaican man with dreads and looked rough. All that was missing was his accent. He gave me a simple head nod as he looked me over and then turned his attention to Cindy.

"Aye, baby, we're going to drop off Gyan first."

"Ight." Was all he said as he grabbed a bottle of water out the fridge and headed to the door. Cindy was so smitten by this man and I couldn't figure out why.

From all our conversations, she was always crying about how he cheated or was disrespectful to her. It was why she decided not to move him into her apartment. From the way he stared at me, I could tell if I wanted to flirt with him he would entertain it. As much as I wished he wasn't moving in, it was something I had to deal with. Who was I to tell her who she could have in her place?

"See you later, Golden. Get some sleep too," she told me.

"I will," I yawned as I locked the door behind them.

After I showered and made some breakfast, I got comfy on the couch and went to sleep. The time for me to head to my second job would be here before I knew it. Sleep was exactly what I needed right now. I said a quick prayer for better times and then drifted off to sleep.

2

Hazel

"Yolani, you need to get up, so we can head to your brother's house. He's been calling you for the last three hours and I'm tired of hearing your phone ring off the hook." I shook my wife and tried to wake her up.

She grumbled a few words and then put the pillow over her head. "Haze, I'm tired as fuck. Let me sleep, baby."

Pulling the silk sheets off her body, I pulled at her feet until she finally agreed to get up. She sat on the side of the bed with an evil expression plastered on her face. "The fuck, man. I'm tired as shit.

"Too bad. Your brother is having his little memorial event for Ashleigh," I reminded her, and her expression changed.

"Damn, that's today? Why you didn't tell me?"

"Babe, why else would I be in the Gucci store getting you a white button-up shirt? The shower is running, and I put the heated floors on too, hurry up." She stood up and stretched before she walked over to me and kissed me on the forehead.

Yolani was my entire world and then some. When we met in

high school, I knew I wanted to be her wife. Well, not automatically, but it took some years for me to figure that out. We were always the best of friends and hung out all the time. At the time, I was into men, and she would always be the shoulder I cried on when they ended up breaking my heart. It was always Yolani that was there for me when I needed her the most. Our friendship took some hits, but through it all, we both remained true to each other. When we graduated high school, I tried my hand at college and realized it wasn't for me. I started doing nails out of my parent's basement and Yolani was there to support me. All the chicks she would mess with, she would make them get their nails done by me and then told me to charge them twenty-dollars more than it cost.

After my ex-boyfriend cheated on me and had a baby, I was done with dating. I enrolled in nail school and got certified. Yolani was right there for me the entire time. I started to develop feelings for her and never told her. How could I have ignored this woman that had been there for me when no one else was there? Each fall I took, she was there with her hand to help lift me up. My parents were proud of my accomplishments but would have preferred college over nails. Each chick that Yolani dated, I always nit-picked. I told her that she deserved better and that this chick just wanted her for the money she had. It was no secret that Yolani was a bully in these streets. I mean, she learned from the best; her big brother, Yoshon. The Santana name and guns ran in the same circles. There wasn't a street soldier with a gun that didn't get it from the Santana siblings. Because of her name, money, and cars, chicks wanted her. When she broke up with her girlfriend at the time, it was now or never.

I had to speak up and tell her how much I loved her, that I had always loved her and never said anything about it. Our friendship meant more than getting into a relationship that could possibly fail. So, instead of telling her how I felt, I hid my feelings and got into another relationship. I continued to be quiet about my feelings until Yolani told me how she felt. She told me how she loved me since the day I walked into her homeroom class. She went on to explain how she wanted to be with me but didn't want to fuck up our friendship. That night, I made love for the first time in my entire life.

Then, I had to deal with the fact that I had a man willing and ready to give me the entire world. Yolani had my heart and she knew it. Fast forward four years and we've been married for exactly a year. The first year was hard. Yolani was a hoe and she loved to get around. I can't count how many times I've had to pull up on her and show her that she married the right one. It took all of five minutes for me to pull off my jewelry and beat a bitch's ass. Eventually, she realized that I wasn't the one to fuck with and stopped fooling around. So, I liked to think she did. There were rumors and I wasn't a fool. The proof was right in my face, and I sat there and listened to her tell me how those women were lying.

"Damn, you couldn't put the heat on?" she complained with the towel wrapped around her.

"Just hurry and get dressed. You know Yoshon hates when we're late. I don't feel like being lectured."

"Yeah, I got you. Make me something to eat," she called behind me as I walked downstairs to make her a quick sandwich.

Yolani was twenty-six and I was about to turn twenty-five. I've always been smart and had skipped a few grades. It was the main reason my parents were upset that I chose to paint nails instead of going to college to become a doctor. Yolani was the only person who knew how passionate I was about doing nails. For my twenty-third birthday, she handed me the keys to a retail space. It was then that *YoYo's Nails* was created. I had to thank her for always believing in me. She never asked to be a partner or asked for money in my business. She just wanted me to truly win and it's why I fell in love with her. My parents didn't agree with my lifestyle and told me that I should have married a man. They told me that Yolani couldn't give them grandchildren and I needed to get over this phase in my life. Loving Yolani wasn't a phase in my life. I loved my wife with my entire heart; I just wished my parents and Yolani understood just how much I loved her. My love was real and it wasn't a joke.

"I'm surprised you not at the shop this morning." Yolani came downstairs buttoning her shirt.

My wife was so fucking sexy. At first glance, all you saw were tattoos all over her body and they came up both sides of her neck. She had thin pouty lips, that led up to a snub nose. Then her eyes, she had these sleepy eyes that I could never resist. She always made me braid her hair in four braids. Two in the front and two in the back. Yolani was the AG of our relationship and I was the fem. I loved my heels, skirts and anything girly, while she would be caught in men's clothes. She had been through some deep shit that made her the way she was.

"I had my assistant move all my dates until next week. My clients are going to be pissed, but I need the time off."

"Shit, I'm not complaining." She licked her lips as she neared me.

"Oh please, you're never home."

"You already know how it goes." She pulled her Rolex out her pocket and fastened it around her wrist.

"Yeah, I do. I also know that those bitches frequenting the traps need to stop. Those bitches bust heads or something?"

Yolani started laughing and shook her head. "Yo, you was never crazy as fuck when we were friends. Nah, I take that back."

"I wasn't your wife, Yolani. There's no reason these bitches are in your face smiling all up in your face. I don't know what's worse, them doing it or you allowing it."

"You gonna start with this shit now? Like, come the fuck on!" she raised her voice like I gave a fuck that she added some base in her voice.

Yolani knew I couldn't stand these bitches in her face, yet she allowed them to smile in her face and give her little phony hugs.

It was one of the biggest issues in our marriage. I wasn't a fool and I heard the rumors about my wife. There was several that she was messing around with a chick in the Bronx. If I listened or followed up on every rumor that came into my shop, my business would be failing. If Yolani was out there doing me wrong, it was going to come back to me, and she would have to deal with it then. Did I like that I had to worry about other bitches around my wife? I didn't, and it annoyed the shit out of me that she thought the shit was funny.

"I don't give a damn about you raising your voice, Lani. You know what it is and I'm tired of you acting like I'm the one that's crazy."

She grabbed the toast out the toaster and stared at me. "You know you beautiful when you mad, right?"

"Stop trying to switch the subject. I've been hear..." my voice trailed off as she accepted a call in the middle of my conversation. This was the shit that I couldn't stand with her. It was always about business when it came to her.

I could never get a word in because she was always handling business. Yoshon used to be the same way, but when Ashleigh got sick, he stepped back from the streets. He allowed Yolani to handle everything while he made sure his fiancée was good. Once in a while, I wanted Yolani to step back and care for me. Our time together was spent in passing. She would kiss me and then go on her way. All I wanted was for my wife to spend some time with me and make the effort. It didn't take much to make me happy. I would settle for a trip to Burger King if that meant that I got to spend time with her alone without business being handled. It was all wishful thinking as I pulled her sausages out the frying pan and got ready to head to Yoshi's house.

3

Yolani

I HAD to make a few runs before I headed to Jersey to my brother's crib. He knew money always moved, and I had to be the one to make sure shit continued to move. Yeah, I could have relaxed and allowed my team to handle shit while I went to do family shit, but we didn't get where we were by sitting back and letting others run shit for us. My team went hard for me and would make sure shit was on the up and up, but I had to physically lay eyes on shit to be able to go on about my day. Wifey bitched and moaned about the amount of time I spent in the streets. I heard her, and I understood how she felt. Truth be told, I wanted to give my woman the world, and it was the reason I worked so hard. The day I was able to hand her the keys to her new storefront for her salon was the happiest day of my life. The shit felt like I was floating on a high for weeks after that. Seeing her smile was all I needed to continue to make sure she was straight.

Hazel had been my heart since we met in high school. She

tried to act like she liked niggas for a few years until she realized that she was feeling me. I always loved her but didn't want to push shit on her. I wanted her to come to me and admit her feelings for me. Except, Hazel was so damn hard headed and stubborn. She refused to admit how she felt about me until I broke down and told her. A nigga was walking around here while the one I loved was trying to find love in all the wrong niggas. Hazel always thought each nigga she dated was the one, until she ended up crying on my shoulder about how they did her wrong. When me and Hazel made shit official, she was still busting her ass and doing nails out her parent's basement. My baby had too much talent to be doing nails in a basement. It was then that I knew shit was real between the both of us. I couldn't see myself without Hazel.

After I bought her salon, I wanted her to move in with me. She refused because she didn't have a ring. Her folks were old school and wanted her to do shit the real way. They wasn't all for her being with a fly ass bitch like myself, but I ignored their judgment. I've been judged my entire life and hearing it from them didn't do shit to me. I put a ring on her pretty ass hand and then we got married soon after. We moved into our crib and been doing this shit together ever since. I loved the shit out of my wife, but her nagging got on my damn nerves. She didn't understand that bitches came with the territory. They were gonna be on a nigga because I had money, was fly and knew I could eat the hell out some pussy. I've turned some of the straightest bitches gay with my tongue game. It wasn't like I was out here cheating on her or anything like that. All I was doing was getting to the money like I've been raised to.

My pops turned his gun on my moms and spilled her brains on my pink carpet.

It was then I said fuck the color pink, fuck this carpet, fuck these pigtails and fuck my pops. This nigga took the woman he married and had children with, away from me. My mother meant the world to me, and when he did that, shit was never the same—for me at least. I went through a tough time mourning the death of my mom's. My grandmother came to the states and did what she had to do to raise me and Yoshon. She came from Belize with barely any money and now had two mouths to feed. Yoshon did what he had to do and put his feet to the ground and got to the hustle. He hustled until his hustle paid off and opened other doors for him to continue to hustle. We went from drugs to moving guns that the military didn't have access to. We supplied some of the most ruthless bosses in New York. The McKnight and Garibaldi empire was our biggest clients. We broke so much bread with them, they considered us family.

When I turned seventeen, Yoshon felt it was time for me to step into the business. He trusted very few, so the fact that he brought me on told me what I already knew. It didn't take me long to learn everything I needed to learn about our business. Yoshon wasn't just trying to drive in foreign cars and have endless amounts of money. He instilled in me that he wanted to create generational wealth for our future kids. I didn't see myself having any seeds, but the fact that he wanted to do that for my future nieces and nephews made me grind harder. He always told me to look at The McKnight's. They had money for their grandchildren and great-grandchildren.

"Are you serious. Today is Saturday and you're about to work. Ugh," Hazel sighed and folded her arms across her chest.

Hazel was beautiful in every way imaginable. She stood around 5'3 with light brown skin. In the winter, she was pale as hell, and in the summer, she would become this golden hue that was beautiful. She had long brown hair that stopped in the middle of her back, cat-shaped eyes and a pouty set of lips that she loved smearing all that Rihanna shit on. Petite was an understatement when it came to Hazel. I called her my Little China Doll because she was so damn small. When it came to that mouth, you would have thought she was over 6ft tall. Her ass could argue you the hell down until she was blue in the face. It was the reason I usually shut down when she kept coming at me with the bullshit.

"Chill. I'm just checking on shit and then we heading to Yoshon's crib. Don't start that shit, Haze," I warned, and she rolled her eyes.

"All I'm saying is that I took off on the busiest day to spend time with family. You could do the same thing."

"Why the fuck you always coming at my neck? If you take off, you got like ten nail techs that can hold it down. I got about two solid niggas I could trust to hold shit down. One is doing a four-year bid, and the other is in the ground. Chill the fuck out!" I barked, and she slammed her back into the leather seat and kept her hands crossed.

Killing the engine, I passed her a burner and got out to head into the trap house. When I walked in, niggas was playing the game and chilling like this was what they got paid to do. Soon as they saw the grimace on my face, they stood the fuck up and started stuttering.

"Oh, oh, oh, cat got your fucking tongue," I mocked them and put a hole in the nigga in the corner. This nigga was so consumed with lacing his blunt with dust that he didn't even see me enter.

"Yo! Yolani, you fucking wilding!" I heard Grape's voice behind me.

Turning around, I put the gun down on the table. "Nah, these niggas always think it's a fucking game when I come through here. When I killed your cousin, did you think I was a fucking joke?" I questioned the nigga shaking in the corner.

This trap was the one that brought in the least amount of money. Not to mention I had to pay off some of our detectives on the force to avoid getting it raided. We moved spots three times and niggas were always getting robbed in this one. I didn't need to stop at the others because I already knew they were going to be good. The soldiers I picked and placed there were going to make sure the traps were held down. It was this one that I spent all my time at, and I was tired of these niggas taking me as a fucking joke.

"Clean this shit up and make it disappear. Let this body be found and you all will be the next," Grape sternly told them as they scattered around like roaches.

"Y'all niggas are out here playing kid games in a grown man field!" I continued to yell. "This trap should be making as much, if not, more than all the other ones and y'all slacking," I continued.

Grape shook his head and nodded his head, so I could follow behind him. "You need to stop being a hot head, YoYo." It was only a select few that could call me YoYo.

"I'll stop when these niggas get their shit together. Until then, I'm gonna continue to be me. I can't even go chill with fam because I'm stopping here to check in on shit. That should never be."

"I hear you. I'm shutting this one down," he revealed.

"Who said?"

"Now, you know I don't need permission to run business. I'm saying that it needs to be shut down. This shit brings in barely twenty thousand a month and it's making it hot for the ones that bring in triple that amount. It was clear that they couldn't handle all the pressure after Big Ben got knocked."

"You right."

"Speaking of which..." he allowed his voice to trail off. I already knew what he was about to say, so I beat him to it.

"I'm gonna go up and see him soon."

"YoYo, you ain't seen him the three years he been in there. Making sure his fam and books are taken care of are enough," he lectured me.

"I hate seeing my nigga down like that."

"It happens. Make your way up there. Big Ben knows you, so

he ain't hurt or anything, but you need to go and have a talk with him."

"I will. When you want to close this hellhole down?"

"Burning this shit down with these niggas in it. Can't have them talking and running their mouths. They already knew, blood in and blood out." He dapped me and headed to his whip. "I'm heading to Yos's crib, so you need to be heading your ass there too."

"Got you." I nodded and went back into the crib. "Stop. I need to say a prayer with y'all." I told them.

These niggas were about to die tonight so I needed to pray for their ass. They knew what it was when you got down with the Santana's. "Pray? The fuck?" One of them questioned, confused.

"Nigga, did I fucking stutter? You Muslim or something?"

"Nah, nah, nah," he stuttered and came to the circle as I stood in the middle.

"Father, watch over these nig... men as they make the trip to you. Make sure they have enough snacks, and if they're going to hell, then I won't question your decision. Amen." They were all staring at me, confused as fuck.

"You acting like we 'bout to die tomorrow or something," the oldest one chuckled as he went to continue wrapping the body up.

"Shit, you never know when the Lord may call you home," I got all spiritual and shit. "Oh, go ahead and put that body in the backroom."

"Word? Thank you, Yolani. I sure didn't feel like driving to Delaware to dump this shit," he sighed in relief.

"Don't mention it." I headed to the door. "Oh, God loves y'all." I left with those parting words and laughed as I headed to the car.

Hazel was on the phone and ended the call when I got into the car. "You ready now?"

"Who the fuck you was talking to?"

"Why?"

"You hanging up soon as I get in the whip. Who the fuck was it, Haze?"

"It was one of my clients. She wanted to make sure I confirmed her for an appointment," she explained. "Damn, you all in my business."

"You ain't got no damn business. The day you married me it became our business."

"Whatever. Can we go? I know Pit Pat making her bomb ass macaroni salad," She smacked her lips as she thought about the food that my grandmother was making today.

"Greedy ass!" I joked as I started the car and pulled off. I knew I was more than a few hours late, but Yoshon knew that business came first and that my lateness was justified.

4

Yoshon

"You always arriving to a function late as fuck," I took a pull from my blunt and passed it on to my nigga, Grape.

Yolani and Hazel arrived damn near three hours late. Grape had showed up two hours ago and told me everything that went down at the trap house. I wasn't in the streets like I used to be, but I had my eyes and ears out there handling shit for me. Grape had been my nigga since elementary school. We did everything together and made a lot of money too. When I first started getting money, I brought Grape on. He too came from a household where his grandmother was raising him and his little sister. See, Grape's sister was twenty and in college. After his grandmother passed away, it was up to him to make sure his sister was straight. He made sure he stayed on her ass for school and now she was in medical school. I wished Yolani would have pursued college, but she wasn't into that shit like that. Soon as I saw her acting out, I pulled her under my wing and showed her the family business. It kept her more than busy and she had showed me some things that could be useful to the business.

"Money always calls. You already know I wasn't going to come until I checked in on shit," she replied and plopped down in the seat next to mine.

We all sat out on the balcony and stared at the lake behind my crib. This was one of the reasons I bought the crib. When I had the weight of the world on my shoulders, I would come out here and smoke some herb to mellow my mood out. Today was the day that I buried my fiancée. She died three years ago from cancer. The shit hit me hard each time I thought about how much I missed the shit out of her. We were supposed to move into this crib together, get married and then fill this crib with children. Instead, it was just me and my grandmother, Pit Pat, that occupied this six-bedroom, seven-bathroom crib. On the day that she died and her birthday, I always put flowers on her grave and let some balloons up for her.

"It ain't always about the money. Some shit is worth more than money and I'm tired of telling you that shit," I reminded her.

My sister reminded me so much of myself when I was her age. Money was the motive, and I didn't give a damn about anybody when it came to the dead presidents on that green cloth. It was plenty times I played Ashleigh to go and chase paper. While I was so busy chasing money, my girl was about to walk out the door on me. She didn't give a damn about all the money I was out trying to make for us. She cared about me and I was letting her down by always answering the street's calls. Yolani had a wife, and she constantly ran the streets like she didn't have a woman at home that loved her. It was a constant issue in their relationship and Yolani liked to push it off like Hazel was the one tripping.

"Man, I gotta mortgage and shit to pay. It's always about the damn money."

Pit Pat always said she was just like our mother. Stubborn, determined and feisty. "You need to stop running every time these niggas call. Trust that I hired a good enough team to take care of shit."

"Those knuckleheads can't handle shit."

While Yolani loved to focus on the trap houses we had around the city, I focused on the bigger picture. I had warehouses and offices around the city and some in New Jersey where I was conducting illegal business like it was legal. I had men that served in the army, housewives wanting to be safe and a bunch of other people that copped guns from us. Yolani wanted to cop work from the McKnight's and start supplying that so I supported her. Drugs wasn't where I made most of our money, so I didn't get her anger when she vented about the traps. A nigga wasn't stupid and made sure to make legal moves too. I owned four McDonalds, three gas stations, two 7/11 convenience stores and a tanning salon. White people loved to tan the shit out their skin. Not to mention, I had a few condos in the city that I bought that I just used to rent out on travel sites. These people paid bank to stay in a condo right in the mid of the city or Brooklyn. Still, I was lowkey and didn't stay showing my face in the hood. The only time I came to the hood was for the monthly meetings that Yolani wanted to hold. I showed my face so they knew that I backed my sister.

"Sorry we were late," Hazel came out onto the balcony with a plate of food. She sat on her wife's lap. "Pit Pat knows how to make some damn food." She smacked on the macaroni and cheese.

"Y'all always late to something. Shit, you were late to your own wedding."

"Shut up," she giggled. "How do you feel?" She stared at me and stopped picking in her food.

"I'm good. Wish she was here, but I already know she ain't coming back. Just gotta keep pushing through."

"Yeah, I know. You do need to get out there and date again, Yos." Hazel always felt like she needed to hook me up.

She tried to hook me up with her workers at the shop and that shit failed. All these women saw was the money and didn't give a damn about me. Was it so hard to find a bitch that didn't want to suck my dick for a shopping spree? The shit pissed me the fuck off and made me not deal with chicks. I wasn't the type of nigga that was just gonna be giving dick out because I wanted some pussy. A nigga was stingy with the dick and only one chick got the dick when I felt like getting some. The only reason she got it was because I felt like I could possibly build with her. Eva was some bomb little chick I had met at the bank. She worked there and would let me in my safety deposit box the few times I stopped by there.

Shorty was concerned about work and wasn't trying to toss her pussy at me soon as I walked through the door. After seeing her a few times, I had gave her my number. We went on a few dates and fucked whenever she came over. Eva wanted more, and I wanted to give her more except I couldn't. It had been six months since we met, and she was pushing to add a label to what we had. Each time the topic was brought up, she would storm out my crib with an attitude. I wouldn't hear from her for a few days; then we would patch shit up and go in the same circle. Pit Pat wasn't a fan of any girl since Ashleigh had passed. She didn't like any woman coming through the front door of my crib. With Eva, she welcomed her with open arms and loved having her around. That should have been enough for me to make her mine. It wasn't. Hazel and Yolani didn't come to my crib often to know about Eva. Pit Pat only met her because she lived with me.

"Nah, I'm chilling right now. When I'm ready, then I'll find the right one," I told her, and she rolled her eyes.

"You over here acting like you young, Yoshon. You're thirty-eight, and you want a wife and kids, how the fuck is that supposed to happen? It's been three years sin—"

"Chill the fuck out, Hazel. You over here pushing the nigga

into a relationship on the anniversary his fiancée died. Chill the fuck out!" Yolani barked and Hazel stood up.

"All I'm trying to do is look out for my brother in law. Raise your voice at me again and I'll beat the shit out of you." She pointed her finger in Yolani's face and walked back inside.

Waving her off, Yolani took a pull from her blunt. "She ain't gonna do shit. More bark than the actual bite," she slumped further down in the seat and pulled on her blunt. "The fuck!" she yelled when Hazel slapped her in the face.

"The bark is pretty vicious too." Hazel smirked and went back inside the house while me and Grape had tears in our eyes.

"You went and married you a feisty one. When have you know Hazel to sit back and let you talk crazy to her?" Grape choked out as he laughed.

Yolani's face was beet red as she sat there with the bent blunt in her lips. "Sis, you need to stop fucking around with her. She ain't those bitches you be fucking with."

"She 'bout to be sleeping alone tonight for that shit. Bet," she vented more to herself than us.

Yolani liked to test the waters when it came to Hazel. She liked to push her and see how much she loved her. The shit she put this girl through was far worse than any nigga she been with. You couldn't be everything for someone when you were broken. Yolani didn't like to admit shit, but she been fucked up for years over witnessing our mother being murdered in front of her. She liked to use the streets as a cover-up and not deal with her feelings. The way she ran the streets for days at a time and didn't return home told me she didn't give a fuck about anything except herself.

"You about to stay out all night because of that?" Grape asked as he rolled another blunt. Yolani straightened out the blunt, put it to her lips and took a long pull.

"She not about to get on my fucking nerves tonight. Once we

leave here, she's gonna be all in her feelings and shit. Nah, I plan to dip out and have someone scoop me."

"Lani…" she heard my voice and waved me off.

"Chill. I'm not inviting no one here. I'll catch a Uber to the city or something." She switched her story.

"Business is good. You can chill for the night; you need to spend time with wifey."

The way she cut her eyes at me, I knew she wasn't going to listen to shit I was saying. Yolani was hard headed and was going to do what she wanted. Hazel had pissed her off so now she wanted to get back at her for pissing her off. If she knew how lucky she was, she would understand that you only got that one person in life that was your first love. Ashleigh happened to be mine, and it took for her to become sick for me to see that the streets don't give a damn about your family or your personal shit.

"I keep telling you that what you're looking for isn't in the streets. She's at home and waiting for you to get your shit together."

"Why the fuck everyone wanna preach to me? I take care of her and I'm there when it matters. Hazel ain't all that fucking innocent. Why the fuck y'all think I'm always leaving and shit?"

"Don't matter. That girl is calling out for you to spend time with her. Shit, I'm not even around, and I could see the shit. Kid, don't be so worried about these streets and forget about your home," Grape advised and she continued to pull on her blunt.

Knowing my sister, I knew she wasn't listening to a damn thing that came out of either mine or Grape's mouth. She already had her mind made up and was going to do what she wanted. Hazel or no one was going to switch her mind. She had to want to make shit right with her wife, and sadly, I didn't think she cared all too much to do that.

"I gotta use the bathroom," she sniffled and got up and went inside the crib.

Grape turned toward me and shook his head. "You know you

can pull the plug on this. The only reason this shit is happening is because of you. Your mind ain't been in the streets for some time."

"Can't do this to her. This is all she has and it means a lot to her."

"It ain't all she has. She has a wife at home, wanting her to be there. Yolani is nothing like you, she's a loose cannon who listens to herself. Even I can't advise her without having to argue with her."

"You know she doesn't want me breathing over her neck. You're the best thing to help keep her on course."

"Yeah, but your sister has a mind of her own. What she wants is what she's going to do, point blank. These niggas fear the shit out of her, but they don't respect her. How many more bodies is she going to lay down, when it could be avoided?"

"You're right. Give me some time to think on what I want to do. Right now, it's about family and Ashleigh, not business."

"For sure. How you feeling about today?"

"I'm good. Life moves on, and every day I realize that, although I needed her here, God needed her more than I did."

Grape patted me on the shoulder. "It's hard for us to accept, but the man above doesn't make any mistakes. Trust that he has a plan for you and it'll be unmapped when he's ready for you to receive it."

"Appreciate that, man." I dapped him and leaned back.

We continued to smoke weed, talk and stare out at the lake behind my crib. I leaned back further in the chair and got more chilled from the weed. As I was about to ask Grape something, we heard a glass break and Pit Pat scream. Jumping up, both me and Grape ran inside and saw Hazel standing there with her hand bleeding and a broken crystal plate in her hand.

"What happened?" I asked.

"I'm sorry. Yolani pissed me the fuck off. How the fuck she gonna come and tell me she got business to handle and leave?

We're spending time as a family," she vented as she placed the broken piece on the counter, and then bent down to pick up the broken pieces.

"She cracked the plate with her hand; woman has gone mad," Pit Pat nervously chuckled and came back with the broom and dust pan.

"Sorry, Pit Pat. Your granddaughter irks my nerves sometimes," she apologized and went over to hug Pit Pat. Pit Pat loved the shit out of Hazel, and she could do no wrong in her eyes. According to Pit Pat, it was Yolani that needed to get her shit together, not her. I couldn't say that I didn't agree.

"Haze, just stay the night. It's late and you don't need to be driving back alone. Pit Pat, I'm 'bout to go lay down."

"Okay, baby." She smiled and gave me a hug. "Grape, come on so I can fix you some food to go." She pulled him by his hand.

"I'll get up with you tomorrow, G."

"Bet."

As I climbed the stairs, all I thought about was Ashleigh. How I wished I could be climbing the steps with her up to our bedroom to relax. It got lonely sleeping alone every night and not having someone to call your own. Yeah, I could call Eva over, and she would gladly come over, but she wasn't on my mind, and I didn't feel like pretending tonight. I didn't feel like pretending I wanted to be laid up with her, while my mind was on Ashleigh. Peeling my shirt off, I sat on the couch in my room and flipped on Netflix. After scrolling for some time, I settled on a documentary and soon after, I fell asleep.

5

Golden

IT HAD BEEN a month since I moved in with Cindy. Things were going great until Darian moved in to the apartment. The vibe went from stress free to stressful. The nigga lost his job so all he and Cindy did was argue. My baby went to sleep with his hands over his ears every night. It made me consider if sleeping the car wasn't so bad. The only time it was quiet was when either Darian or Cindy left. She left for work and he left to run the streets with his homeboys. When he didn't come home at night, Cindy stayed up all night crying in my arms about him. When I left my drama, this wasn't what I signed up for. All I wanted to do was to work, stack my money and move out as soon as I could. Instead, I was stuck cooking, cleaning and trying to make sure my son was good while we lived with two grown adults.

Cindy worked as much as I did and when she was off, she spent her time pampering herself. The laundry, dishes or anything else that needed to be cleaned wasn't a concern to her. I was struggling with picking up the slack of her household and trying to work two jobs. In my heart, I knew I needed to accept these conditions because it afforded us a warm place to sleep at night. Gyan was so excited and happy to have somewhere that wasn't the backseat his home. I tried my hardest to make the best of the shitty conditions I was subject to. All I dreamed and prayed about were the days I wouldn't have to depend on anyone. The day I could provide for my son without having my hands out to anyone else.

"Hey, Gold, what you doing home early?" Cindy came out the bedroom dressed in her Target uniform.

"The pipe burst at work so they sent us all home. I'm pissed because I could have used the money from today."

Clearly, my issues wasn't her concern because she popped some candy in her mouth and grabbed her purse. "Darian is asleep in the bedroom. He had an interview and he's exhausted, so please tell Gyan to keep it down."

"He had an interview, he didn't work a shift," I replied, confused on what being exhausted had to do with going to an interview.

"You know how it is when you're job hunting." She headed to the door and then stopped to turn around. "Oh, and he said that Gyan broke his PlayStation 4. Something about it making funny noises."

"Bullshit. I watch Gyan each time he plays. He is careful with it and I don't allow him to do anything extra on it."

"He was playing it the night you worked late."

"And who's fault is that? I told you that he's not to play with the game when I'm not home. Especially since that night was a school night."

"W...well, he wants the money for it or for you to pay for it be replaced."

"He gonna be waiting on that for the rest of his life. I'm not paying for that shit. Especially not when I told you to not to let him on the game. You either use your discount at Target, or he buys himself a new one."

"We'll talk about it when I come home tonight. Golden, me and Darian are in a good space and I don't want tension in the house."

"Oh, there won't be no tension between me. My son didn't break shit, and I'm not paying for a game system for a grown man that doesn't have a job. The game is the least of his issues," I raised my voice some.

Cindy's eyes damn near jumped out her sockets as she tried to quiet me. "We'll talk about to tonight when I get home," she repeated before she left.

Rolling my eyes, I locked the door behind her and went to the kitchen. After being sent home early, I tried to pick up some extra hours at Target, but no one called out. This was God's sign that I needed to spend the day with my baby boy when he got out of school. Besides the hour we spent watching TV before bed, we hadn't done anything fun. Tonight, I planned on surprising him with some pizza and bowling. It was rare that we did anything fun that caused for me to pay cash for it. This would be a small treat to make him smile.

I sat at the kitchen table watching Maury when Darian came from the back. He stood there with his underwear on and no shirt, stretching like I wanted to see him. Pulling my phone out, I checked my messages and acted like I hadn't noticed him.

"You didn't make me none? Damn, you staying in my crib and can't even make me something to eat," he complained as he looked at the stove and my empty plate.

"The fuck am I making you anything to eat? You have two hands right there, so there's no need for me to make you anything."

"You would think because you owe me mon—"

"I don't owe you shit, Darian. That bullshit you told Cindy may have convinced her, but I know for a fact you had your little bum ass friends here the other day. Stop trying to blame my son to get a new game system. Pathetic ass," I rolled my eyes and placed my plate in the sink.

He towered over me and stared at me like I was a damn juicy steak he wanted to devour. "You could just let me fuck and I'll forget all about it." He pulled me towards him by my waist.

Turning around, I slapped the shit out of him and went into the living room. "Don't ever fucking touch me in your entire life. Even if I was a shady bitch, you would be the last person I let fuck me. Nigga, you don't even got a fucking job and you trying to fuck me. Nigga please!" I yelled and grabbed my car keys. Gyan got out of school in twenty minutes and I wanted to surprise him by picking him up. Darian stood there with a smirk on his face as he continued to watch my body.

"You still owe me that bread," he countered and went to the back room.

Soon as I got into my car, I dialed Cindy's number, and she sent me to voicemail. I called her back three more times and each time I was hit with her voicemail. Tossing my phone into my purse, I pulled off and headed to my Gyan's school. With how things ended when she left earlier, I knew she was pissed and needed time. Once she cooled off, I planned on telling her what went down with Darian when she left. That nigga wasn't who she needed to be with and she was. I think Cindy just wanted someone to give her dick on the regular. She was square shaped with no real shape, and guys usually overlooked her. Darian got the right one because she allowed him to do whatever he wanted, and she just tolerated the things he did for the sake of some dick. It wasn't that much dick in the world that could make me turn a blind eye to a no-good ass nigga. Hell, I was married to rich dick, and I couldn't and didn't turn a blind eye to the shit he was doing.

Cindy just wanted a relationship where she could build with someone. Darian wasn't the man for her to do that, and she acted like she didn't know. Deep down, she knew that he wasn't right for her and that she couldn't have a family with him. Their relationship would always be stuck in one place with no room for growth. He would never be able to travel to all the countries she dreamed of visiting, have children and buy a home. She wouldn't be able to have that because he was content with her paying all the bills while he sold what little weed he got on consignment from his cousin. Soon as the money hit his hands, the nigga was either drinking or smoking the shit up. Not to mention, he had a record, so he couldn't even get a decent city job. So, how was she going to build and have a life with this man? Simple, she couldn't.

"Is everything alright? Did you get fired?" Gyan questioned as he climbed into the front seat of my car.

"Dang? You gotta think the worst happened? I just wanted to pick you up from school today, that's all."

"Can we afford that?" Was his next question. It truly made me see that my son had to grow up sooner than I wanted him to. Instead of being happy his mother was picking him up from school, he was worried about if I got fired or if we could afford the time I took off work. It was sad and it bothered me.

Touching his face, I smiled. "Gyan, I'm the parent, remember? Any decision I make will always be for the good. It may not seem like it, but it is always for us to be better."

"Okay. Where's Cindy's sister?"

"Cindy's sister?"

"Yeah, she picks me up when Cindy goes into work early." When Gyan explained what Cindy was doing, it further pissed me off. She had caught me off guard with Darian's stupid game system that I hadn't noticed she was leaving early for work when she was supposed to be picking up Gyan.

"Why didn't you tell me?"

"Cindy told me to keep it between the both of us. She said that she didn't want you to worry and she had to work to pay bills too. I just didn't want us to be kicked out her apartment because she couldn't pay the bills."

"Gyan, you need to start telling me stuff. In this whole entire world, all we have is each other. We can't trust other people because they have let us down before. When someone tells you to keep something from me, that means they're being shady, and you should tell me... okay?"

"Got it. Won't happen again, Ma."

"Ma?"

"Mommy is for babies. All the boys in my school say Ma," he further explained.

"Well, I'm not their mama's, I'm yours and I like mommy."

"Okay, Mommy," he mumbled, and I laughed before pulling off from his school. "Where are we going?"

"We're going to get some pizza and bowl. I haven't kicked your butt in bowling in months," I reminded him and he laughed.

"Mom, you always lose and get mad."

"Oh, shush up, boy." I mushed him and continued to drive to the bowling alley. I download a Groupon that allowed us to get enough food and a game of bowling with the rental of the shoes. Tonight, we were going to focus on having fun together and not all the problems we had to face in the morning. It was me and my baby boy against the world, and I was fine with that.

"WHAT THE HELL?" I sucked my teeth as I messed with my key in the lock. It always got stuck and then I had to knock on the door for someone to let me in.

Banging on the door as I held Gyan's heavy self, I waited for Cindy to open the door. Gyan had bowled and played arcade games while stuffing his face with pizza. He did it until the place closed and then he made me promise to take him back. Seeing the look on his face told me that I needed to do this more often. As a kid, he needed to do more fun things, and as his mother, I needed to make it happen for him. On the ride back home, he talked about school and his teachers until he fell asleep. I carried him a block to Cindy's building and up the stairs since the elevator was stuck on the third floor. My back and legs was killing me, and I just wanted to lay him down on the couch and catch my breath. Not to mention, it started snowing, and the radio was talking about the mayor possibly closing schools because of some cyclone bomb. They named the storms after anything these days. Either way, I was grateful to have a warm and safe place to ride this storm out in.

The doors jingled, and the door was opened. Cindy stuck her head out the small crack and looked at me with disgust on her face. "You can come and pick up all your things in the morning. I tried to be a good friend and allow you to stay here, and you go and try to fuck my man."

"What? I didn't try to fuck Darian. Cindy, you know me and know that is not how I move. Why would I do that?" My heart was beating out of chest so hard in fear.

"Golden, you never have a nigga, and I've been watching how you walk around him. He told me everything. If you didn't have the money for the game that was fine, but to offer pussy... you're a filth."

"I swear on my son's life that he came on to me. He touched me and wanted to have sex with me. It's snowing and supposed to be a storm, what am I supposed to do?"

"Hold on," she sighed and closed the door and then opened it. Pushing the plastic bag with our blankets and pillows toward me. "You can come in the morning when Darian is at his interview to pick up your stuff." She shut the door in my face and tears poured down my face.

What was I supposed to tell Gyan? He wouldn't understand all of this. All he would understand was the fact that we weren't able to stay in Cindy's apartment and we were back to sleeping in the car. At this moment, I felt like a failure and a shitty ass mother for letting the one person I was supposed to protect down. Bending down, I grabbed the plastic bag and headed down the stairs. Cindy might have had a valid reason if it was any other person. Except, it was me, and she knew I wasn't like that at all. Darian was the one who had cheated on her with his baby mother. Still, it was easier to point the blame my way, instead of facing the reality that her nigga was no good.

We barely made it back to the car because of how hard the snow was coming down. Gyan was a heavy sleeper, so he slept the entire way back to the car. Popping the locks, I sat him in the front seat and then got into the driver's side. Pulling away, I found a secluded block and left the car on for a while. I didn't want to put more gas into the car tomorrow, but we needed to be warm through the night. The house across the street had a little traffic, but everyone seemed to be in their own world and not paying attention to my car in the back of the block. Every night we slept in this car, I prayed that no one found us or called child protective services on us. My son was my world and I don't know what I would do if something happened to him because of me. When Teri suggested I move back to New York, it seemed like the best fit. My grandmother would have welcomed me and my son in with welcoming arms. It seems like soon as I entered New York, nothing went right for me.

I couldn't afford the apartments here, my grandmother was dead, and we were sleeping in our car for the entire six months we've been here. Now, I could add that my only friend accused me of trying to sleep with her boyfriend and tossed us back on the streets. Tomorrow, I didn't plan to make her believe me or see my side of things. Cindy's mind was made up, and she was going to believe what she wanted for the sake of keeping a man beside her every night. Although she did me wrong, I was going to allow Karma to do his job and pray for her. Hopefully, she woke up and realized that the man that she loved so much wasn't worthy of her love. Pulling Gyan's blanket over him, I reclined my chair back and wrapped mine around me and checked my surroundings before closing my eyes to get a little sleep.

6

Yoshon

"WHY THE FUCK did I have to come to Brooklyn in the middle of a storm for this?" I slammed my hand on the wooden table. It wobbled and the fear in all our street soldiers' eyes doubled.

I wasn't the type that liked to throw around my position and act like the boss. That wasn't me and I liked to play low-key. Apparently, these niggas thought it was okay to take money out my pocket like they were handing out free money out here. Yolani called me to have a meeting with them tonight because we couldn't afford to continue to lose money. Drugs wasn't where I got the majority of our money from, but that didn't mean I had money to keep throwing out when I re-upped. This was Yolani's business and it was something she took pride in. They had to set one of our traps on fire and then another one got hit. These niggas didn't even look like they put up a damn fight. If I didn't know better, it seemed like they helped load the shit up for these niggas.

"Boss, we didn't know that a hit was coming. We were bagging the work like Yo said and we got hit," the oldest of the crew replied.

"You never know when a hit is coming, dumb ass!" I barked and he cowered in the corner like the pussy he was. "Find me who the fuck is responsible for this shit. For tonight, shut all the traps down. It's snowing, and these niggas will try and hit all of them up. Shut down shop and bring all the work to the warehouse in the city until further notice," I demanded.

They all stood around and stared at me like I spoke Spanish or something. "Tonight, niggas!" Yolani raised her voice and they scattered like the roaches on the walls.

"What you got up your sleeves?"

"We about to pull all traps out the hood."

Yolani stared at me with a grill that would intimidate her team, not me. "What the fuck you mean?"

"We're supplying the hoods with that product and fucking up our neighborhoods. We need to bring the supply to the nice areas where the white folks at. They get higher than we do."

Grape knew me like the back of his hand, and I knew him the same. I didn't need to elaborate because he already knew what I meant. "How the crackheads supposed to get to us? This shit is stupid, if you ask me."

"Just because something is stupid to you, doesn't mean that it's not right. A crackhead will cross the Atlantic Ocean to get a hit. We move, and they'll come... trust," Grape patted her on the back. "I'm heading home. Hit me in the morning and let me know the move so I can put the team on."

"Bet," Yolani said as she sat down at the table. From her expression, she didn't agree with how things were going to be handled from now on. Still, she ran things in my absence, but it was me who made the final call, and if it wasn't me, it was Grape.

"When am I going to get to have a say in shit? You tell me that I run this, and then you come and make decisions for me."

"When you stop calling me, I'll stop making the decisions for you. Go home. Hazel has been calling you."

Standing up, she dapped me. "You good here?"

"Yeah, I'll lock up and head home. Pit Pat made some lasagna," I informed her. "You need to come by and spend more time with the old lady."

"Yeah, I know."

"Drive safe," I said and pulled her in for a hug.

I looked around the house before I got the text message from Eva. She wanted to come spend the night, and after the day I had, I didn't want to sleep alone tonight. After sending her a message back, I stepped onto the porch and lit a cigar. These niggas had me so pissed with the way they were moving. A lot of these niggas were going to find themselves on the unemployment line. In the new houses, there would be my top-ranking generals working there. The niggas that could hold down a simple crib in the suburbs. As I pulled on my cigar, I spotted a car a couple cars down from the house. These niggas had me so mad that I was smoking a cigar in the middle of a snowstorm. I would have drawn my gun except the Spiderman blanket stopped me. Then, a woman turned on her side and kissed a little boy's forehead as she got as comfortable as she could.

Jogging down the steps, I walked over to the car and examined the little boy and woman closer. She had dried up tears on her face as she tried to get comfortable. If she was lying in a bed, she would have been tossing and turning with whatever that was on her mind. Putting the cigar out, I tapped on the window lightly. She jumped up and reached for something in her purse. Holding my hands up, I backed away from the car.

"Chill. It ain't even like that." I assured her. Pointing to the crib I had just come out of, I continued. "I own that crib right there."

She rolled the window down with irritation and fear written all over her face. "W...what do you want?" she stammered.

"You good?"

"We're fine," she confirmed.

"Nah, you sleeping in the car and it's snowing. Let me help you," I offered and she sniffled. I could tell from her eyes that she wanted to continue to cry.

"No, thank you. We don't need your help; we're fine. Just don't call the police and we'll be fine," she told me and rolled the window back up.

Rubbing my hands together, I tapped the window for the second time. Rolling it back down, she had just irritation written all over her face. "I don't know what you think this is. No, I'm not a crack head, and no, I'm not going to sleep with you. Just leave me the hell alone," she snapped.

"Chill, that's not what I'm looking for at all. I want to help you out, on the real. My condo isn't too far from here, let me help you out." Although my crib was in Jersey, I had a two-bedroom condo in the city for nights when I needed to get away from Pit Pat. I loved my grandmother to death, but she could tap dance on my nerves sometimes.

"As if I would go and stay in some strange man's apartment with my child. Man, please get the fuck out my face." Shorty was definitely feisty.

The street light glared on her face and all I saw was nothing but Melanin Magic. She was the color of a Hersey's chocolate bar. Women looked for the perfect lighting to get the kind of glow she was giving me, and all she had was a dim and dingy street light. When she spoke, I caught a glimpse of her teeth, and they were perfectly aligned with each other and white. Her hair was pulled into a messy bun with a few pieces hanging in her face and in the back. Her diamond shaped eyes were a golden hue. The light shined right into them and they gave off their own light of their own.

"Ma, I can't go home and climb into my bed knowing you and your seed are sleeping in a car," I replied.

"Act like you didn't see it then," she quickly snapped and rolled her neck. "I don't need you standing here trying to help me. Nobody has ever helped me without wanting something in return."

"Then you ain't been meeting or hanging with the right people. Look, I have a condo not to—"

"Awh, shit! Please don't tell me this shit!" she slammed her hand on the steering wheel and messed with the keys in the ignition. "I just got something fixed on this piece of shit," she vented to herself.

"You definitely can't stay out here tonight. Your window is open and you both will freeze before the salt trucks make it around."

"My window would have been up if you didn't keep harassing me. Just leave us alone."

"Bet. I'll just call child protective services in the morning. Little shorty don't deserve to be out here in this cold. He's fucking shivering," I raised my voice.

Stepping out the car, she stared up at me, and it was then that I noticed lil' mama was thicker than a snicker. The leggings she wore were practically clinging to her thick thighs and ass. "Who the fuck do you think you are telling me what my son don't deserve!" she yelled and pointed her little chipped nail in my face.

"Here. Take my wallet and look at my address and all my information. Take my keys and you can drive us there." I dug in my pockets and shoved everything into her hands. "Wait, here take my gun too. I stay strapped, so I didn't want to alarm you."

She stood there with everything in her hands and was still skeptical. "Just drive us to a laundry mat. He can sleep on the chairs while I wash his clothes for school tomorrow," she instructed.

"Ma, you don't see the weather. Ain't gonna be no damn

school tomorrow. Let me take you to my crib and I promise I'll leave."

She fought with her decision as she stared me up and down. "Mom, turn the heat up, I'm cold," her son mumbled and pulled his blanket further up on his body.

"See..." my voice trailed off.

"Can you bring me back to my car tomorrow morning? And I'll call 911 if you try something. I'm very good with descriptions," she threatened me.

"You got it. Come on, grab your stuff and get into my car." I helped her grab their things and picked up her son. She watched me like a hawk as I placed him gently in the back of my Tesla.

"Get inside; you're shivering yourself." I walked around to the passenger side and held the door open for her. When she slipped inside, she leaned back and closed her eyes briefly.

Hopping in, I hit the button to start the car and let the car heat up. When the heat came to the vents, I could of sworn I heard a moan escape from her lips. She rubbed her hands together and then rubbed her thighs. Staring at her, it made me wonder how such a beautiful woman ended up in a situation like this. Women and kids were homeless every day, but with her, she seemed like she was kept. As if she came from money or had money in the past. Something about her didn't rub me that she had been struggling and ended up homeless.

"I have a condo in Prospect Heights. It's two bedrooms, you can use either bedroom, and I'll let you both stay there alone tonight... cool?"

"I... I don't usually do this," she broke out with tears. "I don't get into men's cars and stay in their condos with my son. That's not the type of woman I am, I swear. I literally have sixty dollars to my name to last me until next week." She sobbed into her hands.

I looked between her and the street. "I'm not judging you, Ma. I'd rather it be my car and condo then some of these other niggas.

I'm not trying to ask for anything in return; I just can't go lay my head down knowing that you and your seed was sleeping in the car tonight. Look at it as you helping me out."

She laughed.

"See, you laugh. We would still be going back and forth in the snow if your son didn't say he was cold. I could tell you love and value your son; you're not going to hear no judgment from me."

"Thank you." Was all she said. "I can pay you back when I get paid."

"I told you, I don't want no money from you. All I want is for you and your son to get a good night's sleep."

"Okay. We'll be out your hair in the morning."

"We'll talk and sort this shit out in the morning. Sit back and enjoy the heat, ight?"

"Thank you."

"You don't have to keep thanking me. My grandmother would put me over her knee if she knew I walked away from you tonight."

"Her knee? I highly doubt that."

"Oh, you ain't never meet my grandmother then," I shot back.

"Grandmothers."

"Yeah, but I wouldn't be who I am if it wasn't for mine."

"Mine raised me to be this smart mouth woman who didn't take nonsense from no man. Somehow along the journey, I lost myself."

"People never lose themselves; they hide themselves. Don't know your story, but whoever you were with had you hiding. You never lost yourself."

"That makes sense."

"It does."

We arrived at my building, and I pulled into the parking garage and into the reserved spot. I hadn't been to this crib in over a month. The housekeeper came every week and refilled the fridge with fresh food like clockwork. Although I hadn't been here in a month, she never knew when I was gonna pop up and stay in the city versus my crib in Jersey. She tried to grab her son and I stopped her. Picking him up, I carried him to the elevator and used my key card to access the elevator. She watched as I pressed the 10th floor and sat staring around the elevator. The door chimed when it made it to my floor. We walked down the hall and I let us into my condo. It wasn't something all crazy. It was a two-bedroom condo with two bathrooms with views of a tree-lined street with brownstones. The shit cost an arm and a leg, yet it was quiet and not in the middle of everything, so I bought it.

"This is beautiful. It doesn't even look lived in."

"Don't really stay here. I come here once in a blue, but make yourself at home. There's food in the fridge, cable, and wifi. The bedrooms and bathrooms are down that way. The washer and dryer are in that closet." I gave her a quick tour while holding her son. "Come," I called her to follow me.

I placed her son down on the king size bed in the guest bedroom. She watched and then came and took his coat off and put him under the covers to warm up. Kissing him on the forehead, she followed me out the room.

"I really appreciate you doing this for me. I don't know how to thank you for this."

"Shorty, you don't need to keep thanking me. Get some sleep and we'll talk in the morning. I'll have my guy come out and look at your whip too."

"Okay," she quietly replied and walked me to the door. "It's coming down really bad out there... I don't want anything to happen to you driving in this. You should stay, I mean it's your home."

"I don't want you to feel uncomfortable. I'm good; I'll make it to the crib."

"No, I'm fine. With you, I don't feel that feeling I usually feel when something is off. Can you stay, I would feel like shit if you had to drive in this." she walked over to the huge floor to ceiling windows and pointed to the snow. It was barely visible out there and she was right. Trying to drive to Jersey in this would be a nightmare.

"Ight, I'll stay. I'm gonna be in the bedroom down the hall, if you need anything, let me know." I took my coat off and sat it on the stool in the kitchen. "Try and get some sleep."

"I'll try," she replied as I made my way down the hall.

A nigga was thirty-eight, which meant I wasn't a spring chicken. I had to get me ten hours of sleep or else the next day would be hell. I took vitamins, exercised and ate right when I could. All that no sleeping hood nigga shit wasn't for me. I was one of those hood niggas that needed sleep to function. Closing the door behind myself, I went into the adjourning bathroom and ran a shower. After, I planned on jumping in bed and sleeping until my Pit Pat called to make sure I was alright.

"MY SON WAS HUNGRY, so I made some pancakes, eggs, and bacon," she explained soon as she saw me walk into the kitchen.

The little boy sat at the counter stuffing food into his mouth. It was crazy that this woman was sitting in my crib making breakfast and I didn't know her name, and she didn't know mine. She held a plate up and placed it down on the empty spot on the kitchen island.

"Damn, I appreciate this. I was hungrier than a hostage when I woke up."

"A hostage? That's funny," the little boy smiled as he chewed his bacon.

"Aye, don't you dare speak with your mouth full," she scolded him and turned her back to wash the pots. I admired her ample backside real quick before I returned my gaze to the food she prepared.

"Sorry, Mama," he whispered.

"So, does Mama have a name?" She turned around and smiled.

Wiping her hands off on the dish towel, she extended it to me. "I'm Golden. I'm sorry I didn't mention that yesterday, it was just so much going on yesterday."

"Golden... ah, it makes sense."

"Why does it make sense?"

"The golden hues in your eyes," I explained.

"Never thought about that. My mama named me Golden because I was her gold meal ticket with my father."

"Damn."

"Yeah. This is Gyan," she introduced her son.

"Hi, nice to meet you, sir. Thank you for letting us stay at your house. Will you kick us out too?"

"Gyan Aden!" she raised her voice. "Go place your plate in the sink and go wash your hands in the bathroom."

"I'm sorry, Mama," he apologized again.

"Nice to meet you, Gyan. I'm Yoshon." I shook his sticky hand as he smiled.

"I like your name."

"It's okay. It's not nothing special like Gyan is."

"You think my name is cool?"

"I do."

"Thank you," he gasped and went to do what his mother demanded.

With her hand on her head, she stared down at the counter. "That boy is too much. I appreciate you letting us stay here last night. We'll go get ready, so you can take me to my car."

"Your car needs a new transmission. I had my man go out and get it last night."

"Dammit. Piece of shit car," she muttered to herself. "You can drop us off at a shelter or something. I'm sure you have lots to do today."

"Stop worrying about me. You and your son is straight here. I'm in no rush for either of you to leave. You been up all night?"

"No," she quickly lied. The bags and dark circles under her eyes were evidence that she hadn't slept at all. Not to mention, she was slugging coffee like it was orange juice.

"You know the one thing I hate?"

"What?"

"A liar. I can look past pretty much everything in life, but a liar is one thing I can't overlook or forget about."

"Okay, maybe I didn't sleep last night."

"I could tell from all the used K cups you been using. Go get some sleep and Gyan is cool. You don't know me, but know I would never hurt you or your son. Words are words, right? You got my gun and all the rest of my shit. I'm gonna finish this documentary on Netflix and drink some tea. You can go in the room and get some rest. My housekeeper is home today, so I'll try and cook something."

"Try and cook something?" she choked. "Let me take a hour nap and I'll make some..." her voice trailed off as she looked through the fridge and freezer. "Chili!" She held up the ground turkey meat.

"I'm not gonna argue with that."

"Me either! Can we watch a movie?" Gyan plopped down on the couch and stared at his mother.

"Your moms is tired. She needs to rest. Me and you can watch a movie."

"Please. Don't make him bully you into watching kid movies. Gyan, you need to come lay down with me."

"Ma, he's straight. Y'all have clothes in the car or something?" I noticed they were still in the clothes from yesterday.

"No. It's at my friend's house."

"What size you wear?"

"No, you do—" I stopped sending out a message and gave her

a look. "I wear a size ten in pants and a medium in shirts. He's a size nine in boy's clothing."

"Shoes?"

"We hav— I'm a size five in women's and he's size five in kids." She caught the hint and plopped down on the couch. I sent Grape a message and he told me he was on it.

"What are you, some black businessman? How can you afford all of this?"

"Smart investments."

"I should of made smart investments. I wouldn't be in the situation I'm in now," she muttered.

"Don't worry about all of that right now. Go get some rest and we'll sort this out when you wake up."

"You keep saying that. I'm awake."

"Nah, you sat up all night and didn't get any sleep. You look like a damn zombie."

She messed with her hair and removed it out of her face. "I have to go and pick up my things from my friend. You really don't need to do all of this; we can go to a shelter until I can get another car."

"Ma, who you trying to impress? You were sleeping in your car in the middle of a blizzard. You don't need to front for me. My grandmother raised me and my sister by herself; I know the strength of a single parent, especially a woman. Let me help you. Please."

"It's ju—"

"If not for yourself, let me do it for your son. You think he wants to be in a shelter when he can chill right here?"

She fought with herself as she played around with her hands. I could tell she didn't want help and was independent. It was part of the reason that I wanted to help her. Who else would turn down help in the middle of a blizzard?

"Fine, can you take us to my friend's house? I have to get all of our stuff before she gets petty and tosses it out."

"Let me shower and I'll bring you over there," I told her and went to my bathroom. Shorty was feisty and I liked it. Not to mention, she was independent and determined to do shit on her own.

I had a soft spot when it came to single mothers. My mother was a single mother until she allowed my fuck boy of a father back into our lives. She worked and struggled to make sure we had everything we needed. Although she struggled, we never witnessed it. We just saw our mother coming through with everything we asked for. It didn't always come on time, or when we wanted it, still it came, and she never let me or Yolani down. With Ms. Golden, I could tell she would never let Gyan down.

7

Hazel

LAST NIGHT IT WAS A BLIZZARD, and I sat in my bed with my phone calling my wife the entire night. Yolani never showed up home, and she still hadn't answered any of my calls. Pissed was an understatement. When I called Pit Pat, she thought it was Yolani, so I knew she wasn't over there. Yolani had been my best friend and heart for years, yet she continued to break mine. Not too many people knew we were married and she liked to keep it like that. She told me she did that to protect me, but I wasn't too sure. Yolani was known to keep women around when we were just friends. It was hard for me to believe that she just gave them all up for me. I didn't doubt that she loved and cared for me, I did believe that she wasn't ready to be married. Yolani wanted me and didn't want to make the commitment. She wanted to just call me her girl and live with me, and that wasn't how I was raised.

"Yeah?" I answered my business phone. It distracted me from the rage I felt about Yolani's ass not bringing her ass home.

"Why you gotta answer the phone like that?" Denim laughed over the line. My heart skipped a beat when I heard his voice.

"Denim? How did you get my number?" I gasped and sat up in my bed. It was amazing how I was angry moments before, and now my mood had altered almost instantly.

"I mean, you changed your number when you got with ol' girl... the only way I could let you know I'm back in town was from the number on your shop."

"How do yo—"

"You know my mama was gonna put me on," he cut me off and I laughed.

"So, how are you? How long are you back in town?" Each question spilled out the mouth as fast as the first one was asked.

"I'm back for good. Just opened a sneaker store up in Harlem," he informed me. "Found me a nice ass condo over in Bayridge, Brooklyn."

My heart dropped when he said he was back in New York for good. "W...what made you leave Los Angeles?"

"The shop I opened there is doing good, and it was time to open one in my hometown, feel me?"

"Uh huh... so what's up?"

"Meet me for dinner tonight."

"Tonight? It's snowing outside."

"Snow ain't never hurt nobody... I'm sending a car to come scoop you," he told me and ended the call.

How did he know where I lived?

Denim was the one who got away. He was my ex-boyfriend and we dated for a few months before he moved to California. Denim wanted me to move with him and I declined. It was around the same time that Yolani had told me she loved me. How was I supposed to up and move with her revealing that to me? I couldn't and that's why I told Denim that I couldn't move with him. He didn't get mad or shit on me, he told me that he would always keep in contact with me, and he did. Except, now I was married to Yolani. I couldn't just pick up where we left off when I had a wife.

"The fuck you clutching your phone to your chest for?" Yolani's raspy voice made me jump out of my skin.

Putting my phone back on the nightstand, I recovered quickly. "My phone should be the least of your fucking worries. Where the fuck you been all night?"

"In my damn car. Shit was too damn deep and coming down too bad to keep driving. My phone died too, so you know I was bored as fuck." Yolani messed with her hair when she lied. Right now, she was messing with the tip of one of her four braids.

"Why the fuck do you feel the need to lie to me? You weren't in your car the entire night, Yolani, so why you lying?"

"I'm not doing this shit with you... I'm tired and got a crook in my neck. Why the fuck you wanna start some shit?"

Sucking my teeth, I went right into my closet and started looking for something for tonight. I wasn't going to go with Denim tonight. I had planned to call him back and tell him that I couldn't come, but with Yolani's lying ass carrying her ass in here with a weak excuse, I planned to go out tonight.

"Where the fuck you going?"

"Don't worry about it. You want to walk in here with some weak ass excuse, then I don't need to tell you shit."

In one quick movement, Yolani's hands wrapped around my neck and pinned me to the wall. "Stop fucking playing with me, Hazel. You know what it is with these bitches. They want to fuck me, but I'm not rocking like that with them. Yeah, I was hanging out last night, but nothing happened."

While she was busy explaining, I kneed her in the stomach and then punched her in the chest. "Put your hands on me again, bitch. I'm not one of your little hoes in the streets. I promise you, Yolani, the next time you place your hands on me, I'll kill you!" I was breathing hard as I spit each word right behind the other.

"You got it," was all she said as she left right out the bedroom.

Following behind her, she left out the front door she had come in moments before.

"And don't bring your yellow ass back either!" I hollered as I set the alarm and carried my ass back up to my bedroom.

Yolani had a temper, and when she was upset, she had a hand problem. She had placed her hands on me a total of two times, this being the third. Pit Pat had told her about placing her hands on me and she didn't listen. Her anger problems were an issue and she refused to seek help for them. Being married to a woman in the streets was just as hard as being with a nigga in the streets. Sometimes I felt it was much easier being with a man than Yolani. She felt like she had so much to prove. Going into my bedroom, I made a beeline to my closet and pulled out so more cute clothes for tonight. After Yolani showed her ass this morning, I was going to take his offer and go out to dinner.

As women, we wanted to be cherished and treated the same as when we first got into the relationship. It didn't matter if I was married to a man or a woman, the rules still applied. Me and Yolani never really went on dates because she was so busy. Her idea of a date was to go to one of our mutual friend's party and have drinks together, come home and fuck and then she was right out the door. Sometimes I missed my friend and wanted to spend time with her. It was as if she didn't care or want to come home. I questioned myself and asked myself if it was me? Was I the reason that she didn't want to come home? Grabbing a red bodycon dress, I pulled out a pair of gold heels and the matching clutch. Denim was perfect, and we could have had something. I didn't doubt that I wouldn't be married and in love if I was with Denim. He was a different breed of man.

While other men were scared of commitment, he ran right into it. He wanted someone he could spend the rest of his life with, and I was that woman for him. It was only a few months we had been dating, but he told me that. Then, I had Yolani confessing her entire love to me, so how could I ignore that? If you knew Yolani, you knew that she was far from the type to confess her feelings. I wouldn't have left Denim for Yolani if I didn't feel the same for her. We've been friends for years and my feelings developed way past our friendship. Did I give up years of friendship to be with a nigga I've been dealing with for a few months? No, I didn't, and now I was sitting here picking out an outfit to go and have dinner with the same nigga. It was funny how life worked out for me.

THE DOORMAN to the hotel held open the town car's door for me as I stepped out. I sauntered into the entrance of *The Plaza*. Being married to Yolani, I had never been to anything like this. We've been on vacations and stayed in some of the nicest hotels, yet when it came to being home, we never did nice dinners like this. Denim stood there in the front dressed in a pair of jeans, Balmain loafers, and a velvet blazer. His dark chocolate skin was like a ray of sunshine under the center crystal chandelier. Denim's smile was as big as the Verrazano bridge when he laid eyes on me. His teeth were just like I remembered. White and perfectly shaped. Then, his eyes. Man, his light brown eyes were so beautiful. I remembered staring into eyes as I listened to his dreams. The eyes were the window to the soul, and just by glancing in them I could tell he was a good man that wanted to do right by me. In his eyes, I could also see that he had seen and witnessed some things that made him, him.

Denim stood around 6'4 with a solid build. He didn't have gym rat body, but he didn't have a stomach that hung over his belt. His body was just what it was; solid. My tongue had a mind of its own as it slid out my mouth and then ran over the top of my front teeth. Just staring at his beard had me wanting to sit on his face while he licked me to ecstasy and back. Rubbing his hands, he made his way over to me and smirked when he got near.

"I'm surprised you came. Then again, I already knew you would." He bent down and pecked me on the cheek.

Sliding his hand on the small of my back, he guided me to a restaurant inside the hotel. It was called *The Rose Room*. When we stepped inside, you definitely paid for the ambiance the place held. There was a long velvet couch with individual tables and chairs. The armchairs were velvet and in the color champagne. The wooden walls and curtains made me feel like I was a celebrity. Denim pulled the armchair out and I sat down. He pushed me back in and made his way around the table to the velvet couch. Crossing my legs, I stared him down and admired what time had done to him. He was handsome when he left, yet time did something extra that I couldn't place my fingers on.

"This is real extra... especially for you."

"You live in Beverly Hills for three years; you get accustomed to the finer things in life." He waved over a waiter.

"Bring me your best cognac," he ordered. "And she'll d—"

"I'll do the shotgun wedding," I called out the drink that caught my eye on the thin menu. The waiter scurried off to put in our drink orders and Denim smirked my way.

"So, was it a shotgun wedding? I would ask if you were pregnant, but you know..." his voice drifted off and I giggled.

"You're an asshole, you know that? It sounded good, that's all."

"I bet." He licked his juicy and pink lips. "How you been, Hazel?"

"I've been... good," I uncrossed my legs and crossed them with my right leg. "How about you?"

"Nah, how have you *really* been? Don't feed me no bullshit because you think that's what I want to hear." He was straightforward, like he'd always had been. Denim was never the one to beat around the bush.

"Marriage is tough. We're working on things and trying to be the best we can for each other." What else did he want me to say? Did he want me to say that I was so unhappy that I wanted to scream? Or that my wife felt the need to run instead of talking things out?

"Ma, marriage shouldn't be tough yet. What is shorty doing?"

"Nothing."

How did he expect me to spill my issues onto this fine marble table? My wife was more than likely cheating on me and I didn't know what to do. My shop was doing amazing and from the outside, it seemed like I had the perfect life. I would say marriage, but only a handful of people knew we were actually married.

"Haze," he said my name with this sexy ass grin on his lips.

"Denim..." I repeated. "Tell me about you. What's been going on with you?" It was time to switch gears on his ass. For all I knew, he had a wife and a kid somewhere, and I was over here daydreaming about sitting on his face.

"I had a daughter a few months ago. Me and her moms were together for a year, but called it quits when she was six months pregnant."

"You broke up with her while she was pregnant?" I gasped.

"Nah, she ended things with me. I guess I knew it was coming but didn't expect her to do the shit while she was pregnant with my seed."

"Wow. Do you both have a good co-parenting relationship?"

"Oh yeah, the best one," he accepted the drink from the waiter. "She knows I would do any and everything for my daughter."

"How did she feel about you moving back home?" He watched me as I took a sip of my drink. When I ordered, I was torn on the fig in the drink. Surprisingly, it was doing something for me.

"She knows it's for business and agreed to make the trip with our daughter. Plus, I'm a plane ride back and forth when I need to be." He reached over and showed me the picture of the blue-eyed mixed baby. She was beautiful and from her eyes, I could only assume his baby mama was white.

"She's beautiful, Denim. What's her name?"

"Tailor,' he replied.

"Blue eyes, huh?"

"Her mother has the same blue eyes... Yes, she's white, Hazel," he busted out laughing, as did I.

He didn't have a wife, but he did have a child. How was I supposed to feel about that? We spoke about children and he always told me he wanted them. Hell, I wanted them and told Yolani that I wanted a baby. Each time I told her we should go to a sperm bank, she would panic and tell me she wasn't ready yet. How long was I supposed to wait? I wanted a baby and seeing how happy Denim's baby girl made him, made me want the same. When he spoke of her, his eyes lit up like a Christmas tree on Christmas morning.

"Why you telling me?" I continued to laugh.

"'Cause I see your face. She's not the milk man's daughter," he chuckled.

"She's beautiful. You and her mother made a beautiful baby girl."

"Thank you."

There was a moment of silence and I didn't know what to say. From his expression I could tell he had something to say, he just didn't know how to say it.

"You know I came back for you, right?"

"Huh?" Really? Out of all things to say, I blurted huh like a child being scolded and asked a question. "What do you mean?" I tried to recover quickly.

"I respect your marriage and shit, but you know it should have been me sliding a ring on your finger."

"Don't say you respect my marriage and then follow it up with that statement. Denim, before you left, I liked the hell out of you. After you left, did I still think about you? Yes! Still, it doesn't take away from the fact that I'm married."

"Why keep in touch with me all these years? Yeah, I didn't

have your direct number, but you still kept me on your social media. Why like, comment and check in on me?"

"You did the same for me."

"Why do you think I did, Haze? We were dating for months, but how long did I know you before we started dating?"

"We grew up on the same block. So, who knows?"

"Since we were in fifth grade, don't act stupid. Your parents know and love me, why you fronting?"

"I'm not fronting," I whined.

He wasn't fronting, and as much as I lied to Yolani about how long we've dated, I started to believe my own lies. Denim wasn't a fling over the course of a few months. My parents adored Denim and knew his mother too. Hell, I knew his mother and loved her down. She was a strong Jamaican woman who raised all her boys alone.

"You are. I'm not gonna push it. Just know I'm back and I'm ready to get what's mine. You know what it is," he reached across the table and touched my hand. Electric shocks coursed through my body. You would have thought they lost my pulse the way shocks flowed through my body.

"I'm married."

"And?" he countered.

"You can't... we can't," I whispered. I couldn't do this to Yolani; it would break her. Here I was thinking of her when she clearly wasn't thinking of me. Could I do this to her? The good Lord knew I wanted Denim more than I wanted this drink. Question was, could I?

8

Yolani

"ARGHHH." I sniffed up the white substance that I had become accustomed to. Pinching the bridge of my nose, I leaned back and let the drug take effect on me.

Cherry sat on the right of me rubbing on my leg. She wanted some sex, and right now, I wasn't in the mood. After my fight with Hazel, I came over and finished sleeping over Cherry's crib. She welcomed me with open arms because she was content when me and Hazel got into a fight. Yeah, I could have come home after I left Yoshon at the trap, but that craving for that white powder had me killing my engine in the Bronx, instead of my home. Hazel didn't know about my addiction and she would never find out. Cherry was the only one that knew, and if someone found out, I would put a hole in the middle of her head in broad daylight.

"Damn, move the fuck over." I pushed her over. She was fucking with my high being all clingy and shit.

"Why you gotta be so fucking rude? Ever since your bitch got you upset, you been coming at me sideways," she raised her voice and stood over me.

"Call her a bitch again and you'll be picking your teeth up off the floor."

"Yolani, you always coming for my neck. I've been the one here holding all these drugs in my house and letting you get high whenever you want. My apartment isn't a fucking trap house!" she barked, knowing that the money I paid her monthly was too good to pass up.

"Bet. I got another shorty that will do it for me."

"I'm not saying that you can't... I'm just saying you could treat me fucking better," she switched her tune real quick.

"Cherry, get the fuck out my face. You blowing my fucking high," I complained. I was better off going back to my crib and dealing with Hazel's mouth.

Cherry was once the place I went when I needed to get away from Hazel's mouth. Now, she was becoming like Hazel, and the shit was irritating me. I came here to get high and chill with her fine ass. Lately, she been on my neck and the shit was pissing me the fuck off.

"All I'm saying is that you don't come at your wife that way."

"Get the fuck on!" I barked, and she caught the hint and left me alone. Bending down, I took another hit and then leaned back on the couch and stared at the basketball game playing on the TV.

A nigga wasn't scared to admit that I did coke. I just hid it because I knew Hazel and my brother would overreact. The shit kept me focused and it was something I did when I was stressed. Nah, it wasn't when I was stressed, I had to start my day off with some, and occasionally, I ended my nights with some. Hazel would flip the fuck out if she found out about my little habit. When I did stay home, I usually had to hide the shit and duck off in the bathroom to take a quick hit of it. She never suspected shit and I planned to keep it like that. Hazel knew what I did but she never complained unless it came to the late hours I kept. As her protector, I kept her away from this street shit. Not a lot of niggas knew I was even married and I kept it like that on purpose. In this game, niggas didn't give a fuck who it was. Long as you were tied to the person they wanted to get at, they would kill you too.

I've heard too much about niggas losing their kids and women because they were out in the streets being reckless like they didn't have a family. Hazel meant too much to me, and I could never look her parents in the eyes, if something ever happened to her. My baby was my world and I knew I was putting her through it with the shit I did. It was hard trying to be this dedicated wife when there was temptation everywhere around me. Women were tossing their panties at me like the niggas. Half the time, those bitches weren't even gay, they just wanted to be down with a nigga that had money. Hazel deserved more from me, and I could acknowledge that, still I didn't know how I could give her that. Mentally, I was fucked up and knew I shouldn't have agreed to be in a committed relationship with her.

Part of me was selfish. I saw her getting cozy with that nigga she used to fuck with and I was jealous. She thought she kept their situation on the low, but I knew all about it. One night, when she was over my old apartment, she was on the phone with her best friend, Mo. She was going back and forth on if she should just up and move to the west coast. I couldn't have that shit, especially when I knew I loved the shit out of Hazel. If she moved to the west coast, it was no doubt that her and dude would have made the shit work. It was then that I knew, if she moved, I would ruin any chance I had of ever being with her. Hazel had feelings for me and I knew it. Mo had been put me on and told me how she was scared. She didn't want to ruin our friendship, and neither did I. Hearing her consider moving to the west coast put a battery in my back, and I made my move.

"I'm about to go over to my sister's house. It seems like I'm not needed right now," Cherry's childish ass pouted. I knew for a fact that she couldn't go over to her sister's crib.

"Bring your crybaby ass on over here." I leaned forward and took another sniff before I pushed the glass plate away from me.

Leaned back on the couch with my head leaned back, she crawled and cuddled up next to me. "I'm tired of you acting like this toward me, baby," she whined.

"Yeah," was all I said as the high took over my entire body. It felt like each part of my body was sensitive and numb. A nigga felt her eyelashes were about to float the fuck away.

"Babe, you really need to slow down on that shit. It starts as coke, and then it'll go to crack real quick." When this bitch opened her mouth and let those words spill out, I almost punched her in her gap-toothed mouth.

"With all the fucking money I got, I would never be caught wrapping my lips around a glass dick, you hear me?" I mushed her head and she leaned up from me.

"Damn, you always putting your hands on somebody. My mama did a little coke," she did air quotes and continued. "Then, she fucked around and started doing crack and abandoned her daughters. All I'm saying is that you're breaking one of Biggie's rules; you're getting high off your own supply."

"Bitch, you over here acting all high and mighty when your mama down the block sucking one of my general's dick for a rock right now. Let's not mention how your sister is a fucking dust-head. You don't do drugs, but your ass sure like to drink like a damn fish!" I hollered and stood up.

She grabbed at my pants and tried to make me sit down. "Baby, I'm sorry. I just worry about you." She tried to recover and soothe out that judgment she had in her tone moments before.

"Nah, worry about yourself. Don't be worried about me, I'm gone," I replied over my shoulder as I grabbed my leather coat and car keys.

Here I was trying to spend some time with her because Hazel

was on my nerves and her ass was now fucking up my high. The streets were quiet, and it wasn't shit that I had to do, so I jumped in my whip and headed home. If I knew Hazel, I knew she would be cuddled up under her cashmere blanket watching re-runs of her favorite old school shows. Right now, I could use a cuddle session with my wife while smelling her scent that drove me wild.

Golden

As I SAT in front of this man with a white cotton robe on, I felt so comfortable. It had been a full year since I had soaked in a tub with a bath bomb, dimmed lights and just my thoughts. Gyan was asleep and I didn't have to worry about anything. I still had stuff to worry about, but in that moment, I cleared my mind and relaxed like Yoshon told me to do. When he realized that I wasn't going to take a nap, he settled on a bath. I still put up a fight until he won. This man was a stranger. He could act nice and kill both me and Gyan seconds later. My radar wouldn't allow me to look at him like a threat or like he was dangerous. In my heart, I knew this man was a good, hard-working man. The entire ride to Cindy's apartment, he held an entire conversation with his grandmother. She fussed at him about forgetting to come pick her up to go grocery shopping. My mind couldn't help but wonder why he wanted to help me? There was nothing I could offer him for all the help that he has done for us so far.

"You keep staring. Why don't you get what you have to off your chest?" He broke our silence and caused me to look away.

He was consumed with fixing the Chinese food we had picked up on the way back to his condo. Never did I think he was paying attention to my stares. "Why do you want to help me?"

"Why is it so hard for you to believe that someone wants to help you?"

"Because people don't help me. I'm the person that has to pick herself up and fight for everything she has."

"Well, I'm a person that's helping you. I don't know about the other people in your life, but I'm not them. I was raised to always lend a helping hand and not expect anything back."

"We're not a charity."

"I didn't say you were. If you were a charity, I would have tossed a few hundred dollar bills in your car window and continued home. Stop pushing how you feel about yourself on me." He handed me the plate and sat right in front of me on the armchair.

It was back snowing again, and he had the blinds open, and we watched the snow fall from the sky onto the busy Brooklyn streets. Staring down at my food, a tear slid down my cheek. Wiping it away quickly, another one fell right behind it.

"Don't tell me I made you cry and shit?" He chewed the broccoli and pointed his fork at me. It was something about this man. His appearance intimated me.

"No," I sniffled and wiped away the tears. "What you said just hit me."

"Ma, like I said, I'm not passing judgment on how you ended up here, nor do you need to tell me."

"I'm not giving my all to my son and I feel bad. I'm trying, and I'm trying hard to be a good mother that he deserves."

"You are."

"You don't know that."

"I've spent the entire day with you and you were on him like white on rice. Anything he needed, you provided. When he was nervous about the car sliding in the streets, shorty you climbed in the back of my whip and sat with him. You trying to be a perfect mother will let him down, more than you being an imperfect mother."

"Thank you."

"You're welcome," he finished his plate and brought it to the sink. After rinsing the plate, he sat it in the sink and then leaned on the counter and stared at me. "I'm gonna take my ass home because I miss my bed. Like I said, you're free to do whatever and act like this is your crib. Don't be scared if you see a small Spanish woman cleaning and shit. She comes every morning to make sure shit is straight. If you need anything, let her know."

"Um, can you tell her not to come this week? I can help around and clean up; it's the least I could do."

He debated for a moment before he shook his head yes. "I'll let her come make up her hours at my sister's crib."

"Okay. Drive safe," was all I could say as I walked him to the door.

He pulled his hat over his eyes and exited out the condo. Closing the door behind him, I leaned on the door and sighed. Who would have thought that I would go from sleeping on my friend's couch to sleeping in my car in the middle of a blizzard? Now, I'm staying at a complete stranger's condo, and he wants nothing in return. My phone deterred me from my thoughts, and I rushed over to answer the phone.

"Hey, Teri!" I greeted. It had been a while since we had actually spoke over the phone. I would send her a message here and there and let her know that we were fine.

"Hey boo... how's everything? You were on my mind heavy last night, is everything alright?" Her voice was laced with concern.

"We're fine. Gyan is asleep, and I'm finally putting some food in my stomach."

"Okay. How's things been there? You still have work, how's the car running?"

I could tell her that I'm sleeping in a stranger's condo, the car was a piece of shit that needed more work done to it, and I haven't slept in the past twenty-four hours. Instead, I forced a smile on my face and lied. Why did she need to worry about me? She had her own family to worry about and I was a grown woman. I didn't want to say that I deserved what Grand did, but I did know about his cheating and his grimy ways. I still chose to be with him and then marry him, so I guess I could say I got what I asked for.

"Everything is amazing. My job has been great, and we just moved into a condo. I'm thanking God right now," I continued to pour out this lie.

"I'm so happy for you, Golden. Grand is running around here and puffing his chest out that he's free. He asked me about you and I acted like I didn't know. He's not looking for you, Golden."

"I still don't trust him. He loves his son and I know he wants to know where his son is at. I'm not putting me or Gyan's safety at risk."

"Honey, I understand that. You continue doing you and being an amazing mother to my nephew. I promise I will make it up your way to see you both. I better have a room at this condo," she giggled.

"The guest room is all yours," I lied some more. I've never been big on lying, and now I had become this master liar.

"Okay... let me go and get this dinner started. Mama ain't been the best, so I've been over there helping her out. I'll give you a call next week," she promised, and we ended the call.

I wished I could say my heart went out to Grand's mother. It didn't, and I wasn't going to pretend to send a prayer up for her. That bitch had never liked me, and she didn't bother to hide it. Each time I was around her, she made sure to make me feel uncomfortable. When I had Gyan, she questioned him because he was lighter than me and Grand. My grandmother was light skin, so I never questioned it. She had to be the one to drag it out and make all his family question why he was so light. I didn't wish death on her or anything, but I wasn't going to fake concern when I didn't care.

When I went to get my clothes from Cindy's house, her bum

ass man had the nerve to be there. He watched as I grabbed all my bags and left the apartment, struggling. I had to beg Yoshon to stay in the car while me and Gyan went to her house. I never told him why I was kicked out of my friend's house, but I'm sure if he saw or heard the stuff Darian was saying, he would of probably killed him. Darian was so tickled that he managed to get me kick out of Cindy's apartment and life. Little did he know that I didn't give a damn. I've lost friends I've known longer than Cindy. I prayed she got some sense and cut his freeloading ass off, but I had to pray and keep it pushing for both me and Gyan. I cleaned up the kitchen and then went to climb into bed with my baby boy. He was so comfortable as he laid out nearly in the middle of the bed. Snuggling close, I laid down and let sleep find me.

"GYAN, if we miss this bus, I'm going to be pissed," I sucked my teeth. He was walking slow with his hands stuffed in his pockets. The ground was still icy from the snow that we got last night. The landlords on this block did the best they could to clear the streets. Staring back, I noticed my slowpoke of a son was still dragging his ass. "Gyan, if we miss this bus, I'm not making your favorite tonight."

Soon as he heard those words, he put some pep in his steps and matched my speed as we headed down the block to the bus stop. After using Google maps to figure out how I could get to Gyan's school to drop him off, and then get to work, we were on our way. This morning he dragged his tail for a bit because he claimed the bed was too comfortable. It felt good to wake up and make him breakfast before he had to start his day. In the back of mind, I continued to tell myself not to get too comfortable with this arrangement.

"Why you didn't call me?" I heard someone call out. Stopping mid-stride, I saw a black Mercedes G-Wagon pull up beside us.

"That truck is fire, Mom!" Gyan gawked over the luxurious car.

"I can manage to get my son to school and myself to work. There was no need to pull you out of bed early in the morning." He made sure to make me program his phone number into my phone.

"It's cold, get in the truck," he demanded, and I didn't put up a fight. He hopped out, came around and held the door open for me and Gyan. It was something I noticed about him. The short amount of time I've been around him, he never allowed my hands to touch a door. Even when I didn't allow him to come into Cindy's apartment, he got out and held the door open for us.

"Thank you," I told him and placed my purse down on the floor, put my seat belt on and looked to the back to see if Gyan did the same. He was so into the truck that he didn't make eye contact with me until Yoshon finally got into the car.

"Cold as hell out there. You should have called me," he made sure to mention for the second time.

He was already allowing me to use his condo, what did I look like calling him for free rides to work and school? Certain stuff wasn't necessary. I hadn't lived in the city for a few years, but I could manage to get around long as I could navigate with my GPS app on my phone.

"Listen, I didn't feel the need to call you in the morning. Just because we have to be up early doesn't mean you have to."

"I get up at four in the morning every morning and work out with my trainer. You don't need to ever worry about that. Next time you know," he informed me.

Staring at his body, you could tell he worked out a great deal. Everything was all tight with his veins busting out his damn skin. It turned me on to see a man so fit and conscious about his body. Men these days were so into drinking Sprite with lean or smoking their lungs black. It was nice to see a man who was into fitness. Yoshon was a fine specimen of a man. He had this whole older vibe going and it turned me the fuck on. His brown skin had small moles and freckles around his eyes. His lips, man, his lips were nice, pink and juicy. I wasn't big on kissing, yet I wouldn't mind sucking his lips while I rode his dick, hard. His full beard was a turn on in its self. He wasn't in the trend of the long and thick beards. He had one, but it was cut low. Yoshon put me in the mindset of the rapper Method Man, and everyone knew that man aged like fine wine in a cellar.

"You gonna stop screwing me with your eyes?"

Looking away quickly, I was embarrassed. He had pulled off and was paying attention to the morning traffic. If I knew he was staring at me, I wouldn't have kept my eyes peeled out the window.

"You don't curse?"

"Not in front of children."

"Thank you." Gyan's own father couldn't practice that rule. He would say any and everything in front of our son. I didn't want to make it seem like I was a saint because I was far from it. Still, I tried not to curse when my son was in my presence. *Damn* or *shit* would slip out my mouth occasionally, but I never cursed at or around my son if I couldn't help it.

"Where's his school?"

I rambled off the address and he nodded his head. We drove through Brooklyn, and I stared out the window, glad that I didn't have to tackle that public transportation commute. The snow here in New York City was always different from Virginia. In Virginia, I would stand in my big bay window and watch the white snow trickle down onto the driveway. It would stay white for days and then eventually, it would get dirtied when the kids ran their dirty shoes and shovels through it. Here, it was different. It seemed as if soon as the snow fell to the ground, it was dirty. As a child living here, I remembered just having snow. It didn't matter if it was dirty or clean, it was snow. As an adult, I could see how dirty and nasty the snow here in the city really was. We pulled in front of Gyan's school, and I was about to touch the door handle but Yoshon stopped me.

"Whenever I'm around, you don't ever touch a door, door handle or anything... okay?"

Nodding my head, I allowed him to get out and swagger around the truck. He held the door open for me and I walked Gyan into the school. Kissing him on his cheek, he was quick to wipe it away before anyone else saw. My little boy wasn't so little anymore and he wouldn't need mommy around him forever.

"Have a great day today. I'll be here to pick you up from school, okay?"

"Mom, what ab—" He fixed his mouth to ask about my other job and I shut him down. Gyan didn't need to worry about the adult issues I had. I wanted to keep him a child for however long I was able to.

"Stop worrying about that. Go into school and be a kid, Bighead." I teased and he allowed a little smirk.

"Okay, Mom. Love you." He kissed me on the cheek and then ran into his school. I stood there watching him longer than I needed to.

"You know he's probably in third period, right?" Yoshon joked from behind me. leaning on the car, he stood there with his arms crossed and observed. It was then that I noticed that he had on a pair of basketball shorts, those athletic tights underneath and a hoodie on. His hat was sitting real low over his eyes.

"Shut up, tights," I remarked and got into the car.

"Oh, she got jokes," he snickered and drove away from the school. "You're not going to work today," he told me.

"Wait, what? I have to go to work. If I don't go to work, I can't feed my son," I panicked and turned toward him. I didn't give a damn about the damn seatbelt; this man was speaking pure foolishness right now.

"Don't worry. You'll feed your son," he told me.

"How?"

"Let me worry about that. I gotta make a run to my crib real quick," he told me and ignored my concern and pure panic mode face. "Calm down. I didn't say you wasn't going to work ever; I just said not today."

"Why, though?"

"Because I think I should spend the day getting to know the woman who is staying in my condo... and shouldn't you get to know the man providing the condo?"

"You're right. See, I don't have anyone who can cover my shift."

"Call out. If they fire you, I have a good lawyer. Not like you need to fight for the job you have. It must not be shit if you're sleeping in your whip with a bad transmission."

"It wasn't much, but it allowed me to feed my son." I sent a quick message to my manager and then turned my phone off quickly. She would call me and demand me to tell her over the phone why I couldn't come in to work. To avoid all of that, I shut my phone off and shoved it in my purse as he continued to drive.

"Where you from, Golden?"

"Here."

"I know you're from here. I hear the New York all in your voice. However, I don't hear it in your son's voice. So, where were you living after you left New York?"

"You're either too observant or too nosey."

"It's not every day I help a beautiful woman and her son. And, to answer your question, I observe everything."

"I'm from North Carolina. I lost my job down there and came home to stay with my grandmother to find out that she's in a nursing home and my uncles sold her home. So, that's how I ended up where I'm at now." The lie just fell off my lips like they were the truth. Had I become a liar? He couldn't know where I came from or that I was running from my husband. Grand knew a lot of people especially up north. What if this man knew Grand and tipped him off to me? Teri said that he wasn't looking for me and I didn't believe it at all. To her, he wouldn't mention that he was.

"Damn, I'm sorry to hear about that. None of your family didn't let you stay with them?" he continued with his questions. It was annoying to lie because then you had to remember your lie and try hard not to get caught in your lie.

"I did for a while. We stayed from place to place until we became a burden on them. My family is funny acting, so I chose to stay in my car until I found a place."

"Who house you was staying at before? The project building you didn't let me enter?" God, this man had too many damn questions.

"A friend."

"Friends don't kick friends out during blizzards."

"Her boyfriend tried to have sex with me and I turned him down. Instead of being honest, he lied and told her that I tried to have sex with him."

"Corny ass nigga," he muttered.

"Exactly. I don't blame her. She's in love and is going to do anything to make sure she keeps her man. It is what it is."

"How old are you?"

"Twenty- Six."

"You the same age as my little sister."

"How old are you?"

"Thirty-eight."

"Damn, you damn near forty years old. Where's your wife, minivan, and kids?" I choked out in laughter, glad that he switched the subject because I didn't think I had any more lies in me.

"You think you funny? I don't have a wife, and I would shoot myself before I drove a minivan and I don't have any kids. At least none that I know of."

"Kids are amazing, man. I love my son so much and he has

given me so much purpose in life. Everything you do, you just do just to make their lives better, you know."

"Yeah, I've heard from collogues and friends."

"You're established. Well, it seems like you are. Go out and meet you a woman and have a kid or six."

"If only it was that simple. I'm seeing someone. We'll see where it goes."

We pulled into a sub-division called Bel Air Woods. You had to pass a security gate and then the gates opened, and we drove through a bunch of mansions. These homes were so beautiful and I knew they had to cost somewhere in the millions. I probably looked like Will Smith did in the back of that cab during the beginning of *The Fresh Prince Of Bel air*.

"I thought Bel air was only in California?" I gasped.

"If you have enough money, you can make it come to the east coast," he chuckled. I could tell this wasn't the first time he had mentioned this to someone.

"You wake up here every morning? I could only dream of living in something like this."

"Don't sell yourself short. You don't know what your future holds." He winked and continued driving for a few perfect tree-lined blocks. He turned into a driveway, and we were greeted by a brick driveway and brick colonial home. It was whitewashed brick and the home had two small pillars that greeted you before the huge wooden door. The small bushes were perfectly lined up, and I could tell his landscaper was well compensated for all the work that was throughout the yard.

"This is your home?"

"Yep," he replied and killed the engine. He came around the car and opened my door for me. I almost didn't want to step out because the driveway bricks were so beautifully laid out on the ground. If it wasn't clear before, this man had money, and he had lots of it. "Come on. I know you haven't ate breakfast yet."

"I had a nibble of toast," I admitted. My concern was with

feeding my son, so I never worried about putting the proper fuel into my body. I would grab some fast food here and there, but when it came to Gyan, I didn't play.

"See. Don't even know you that long and I knew you didn't eat. Come on," he grabbed my hands and led me inside the house.

A staircase off to the side greeted us along with a huge marble fireplace further down into what I assumed was the family room. My shoes made noise on the mahogany wood floors as he continued to pull me through the beautifully decorated home. We passed the family room and made a right, right into the kitchen. It was then my stomach growled as I smelled the aroma of the food cooking.

"Pit Pat, I'm back, and I brought some company." He pulled me in front of him.

I smiled at the short woman with gray hair and matching gray eyes. Her beige skin was flawless, and she didn't look a day over forty, so how old was this woman? "Hello, take a seat and let me put something on your stomach," she demanded with a slight twang. From her accent, I could tell she wasn't from here in America.

"Thank you, Ma'am," I told her and took a seat like she told me to do. It was something about older people. You didn't tell them no, you did what they said. It didn't matter that I had just met this woman seconds before, I would oblige her demands because I was raised with respect.

"Ma'am?" she laughed. "Me-lawd-Jesus," she said as if it was one word. "Child, my mami isn't here. Call me, Pit Pat," she laughed and then lifted her cheek so Yoshon could plant a kiss on it.

"Okay, Pit Pat." I smiled.

"What you over here making?"

"Boy, get over there and shush. I'm almost done. I need to know who dis mystery girl is. She's beautiful, Yoshon." She shooed him away and he came and sat down beside me.

"Instead of the condo, you'll be staying here with us."

Pit Pat placed a cup of orange juice in front of me. "Huh?"

"The condo is where I go to conduct business in the city. Not to mention, I rent that shit out on *Air BnB* and I have some bookings I can't cancel."

"You got your hand in everything, huh?"

"In order to never go broke, you gotta work, right?"

"I appreciate everything you're doing, but this is your home. How do you know that I'm some scheming chick trying to get close to you?"

"Your son. That's how I know."

He answered the question right there. I would never put Gyan in no type of harm. "I work, and he goes to school in New York. This is New Jersey."

"You can quit your job. I have a tanning salon and I will give you a job there. Gyan can get driven to school every morning. My gym is in the city and I make the commute every morning."

"This is nuts," I started to stand up, but Pit Pat placed my plate in front of me. "Thank you, Pit Pat," I smiled as she served me first and then Yoshon.

"You're welcome, gurl." She touched my shoulder and then returned with her plate. She sat across from both me and Yoshon.

"Blended beans, fry jacks and eggs," she answered my question before I could ask it. I guess she saw me observing the plate in front of me.

"She's from Belize," Yoshon explained. "It's native from her country."

"What is this going on?" She waved her fork from me and then to Yoshon.

Putting my head down, I replied, "I'm homeless and he has helped me out a bunch. I appreciate all you're doing, but I can't accept this."

"She has a son, Pit Pat," was all Yoshon said. He didn't look at me, he just stared right at his grandmother and then he started eating his breakfast.

"You can, and you will. Being stubborn and proud will cause you to live on the streets with your son. It's settled, she can sleep in the guest suite." As I was about to fix my lips to say something, she cut me off. "The only thing leaving your lips better be that you love my food."

Smiling bashfully, I grabbed my spoon and tasted some of the beans with eggs. This woman stared me down as I took a bite of her food. With all her staring, how could I tell her no? I guess I couldn't, right?

9

Yoshon

PIT PAT HAD a way where she could tell someone what they were doing, and they did it. Since I laid eyes on Golden, she had put up a fight when it came to my help, and here she was submitting to Pit Pat's every word. I leaned on the dresser in the guest suite and laughed when Pit Pat went into the bathroom, rumbling off more instructions.

"You think you're so funny, huh?" she rolled her eyes at me. "Getting your grandmother on me?"

"I had to do what I had to do. It could have all been so simple," I sang as I shrugged my shoulders and Pit Pat returned.

"Now, there's another bedroom that connects to this one. Your son can sleep there and you in here. You both don't need to be huddled up like we're gonna kill you or someting." She pointed her finger at Golden.

"Yes, Pit Pat."

"Okay. I'll leave you be. Yosho, make sure you go grab her things from the condo. Where's the boy?"

"In school."

"Okay. Go with him because I know that's your boy and you'll worry. We got you, you hear?" she wrapped her arm around Yoshon and hugged him tight. "His mama and me were homeless in Belize. No house, no nothing, and nobody offered a hand. I know what's like, mama. Let us help you. I raised a good man here. Nothing in return for helping you out. Let good people help you. Okay?" She grabbed Golden's hand and stared her in the eyes.

This was Golden's test. Pit Pat was huge on eye contact. She always told me the eyes were the windows to the soul. If a person couldn't give a firm handshake or eye contact, they were wicked. Golden stared her right in the eye with red eyes. She wanted to cry, and I knew she did, still, she didn't let a tear fall down her cheek as she stared my grandmother in the eyes.

"Thank you, Pit Pat." She squeezed her hands and Pit Pat smiled before she left the room. When Pit Pat was out the room, Golden rolled her eyes at me. "This was your plan all along? How do you know I'm not casing your place?"

"'Cause I trust my grandmother and she would have told me if she felt something off with you. Like I told you, you're good, and I got you."

"It's hard to believe that when you say it. Nobody helps someone without wanting anything in return." She was so skeptical, and I could see she had been hurt in the past. Her face showed that she was disappointed more than a few times, and skepticism proved that as well.

"I'm not nobody; I'm Yoshon Santana." When I said that, she leaned on the bed with her arms crossed and stared at me. She stared as if she was trying to figure me out or read me

"Thank you. I really do appreciate it and don't know how I'll pay you back. But, if you're going to allow us to stay here, I want to pay you some kind of rent."

"Rent? Ma, I own this crib so what you expect me to do with your rent money?" When I bought this crib, I paid cash. Because I made smart investments, I had the paper trail to show how I was able to afford this house, and where the money came from. Besides taxes every year, I didn't know what the hell Golden wanted me to use her rent money for?

"Okay... so I'll pay for my own food." She tried to find another reason to hold onto her independence.

"That's something you have to work out with Pit Pat; she handles everything that has to do with the kitchen. All I do is eat the food that's on the table when I come in."

Sighing, she tossed her head back. "How can I help around here? I want to earn my keep."

"Clean my room."

"Seriously?"

"Nah. Put all your hard work into the tanning salon. Earn a check and show me I didn't make a bad decision by helping you out."

"Me? A black girl working at a tanning salon."

Laughing, I leaned up from the dresser. "I have some black clients that come in too. We're not all blessed with this chocolate goodness."

"I guess," she giggled. Looking at her watch, she stared back at me. "Do I have time to take a quick nap?"

"Be my guest," I told her and headed out the room.

I went in my room to remove some money out my safe and then went downstairs where Pit Pat was cleaning up the kitchen dishes. When we first moved into the house, I hired a full staff to take care of the crib. She would argue them down and go after to do it her way. Pit Pat was seventy years old and still got around like she was young. Besides a bad knee, she got around and took care of this house. I wanted her to relax and have people cater to her, and that's not what she wanted. She hated to be treated like a baby and told me she was going to be the woman of the house until I bought me a wife home.

"Want some left-over beans?" she called over her shoulders while in the fridge.

"Nah, you trying to have me with gas, Pit." She laughed and turned around with vegetables and seasonings. "What are you about to make now?"

"It's more than just me and you, boy. I need to cook a good dinner... see if you bull-headed sister will come over," she told me.

Growing up, Yolani and Pit Pat always had a crazy relationship. Yolani spent half of her teens trying to figure out who she was. She was struggling with her sexuality and Pit Pat didn't understand. Shit, I didn't understand her, and I was her brother. How could you help someone who was battling with their sexuality and didn't know themselves? You couldn't. Growing up, I didn't know how many times Pit Pat kicked Yolani out on her ass after she disrespected her. Their relationship was better now, and Pit Pat made sure she inserted herself in Yolani's life. If you left it up to Yolani, she wouldn't call or visit us at all. Once she got into the streets, the streets consumed her. Hazel, as her wife, didn't even come before the streets. It was something I constantly told her she needed to work on. Still, if you knew Lani, you knew she didn't listen to no one except herself.

"You know Yolani isn't going to come over here. I'll ask Hazel if she'll come over tonight. You know she loves spending time with you."

"I love spending time with her. Wish my big-headed granddaughter listened to me about her. They didn't need to get married."

"You gotta let her live her life, Pit Pat."

"And look how that turned out. She's in the streets more than you, and she married a girl that she barely makes time for. You know how many times Hazel comes over here and cries to me? She can't go and cry to her parents because they'll just throw it in her face how she doesn't listen. That child wants her wife, not her wife running the streets."

"I try not to get involved in their issues. Yolani likes to share what she wants, and that's it." Whenever Hazel needed someone to vent to, she went to Pit Pat. If it was one person you could talk to without them forming judgment, it was Pit Pat. She could listen, give advice and put you in your place without you feeling judged or scolded.

"Well, that child loves her some Lani. I know love, and when I look into her eyes, I could tell she loves Lani, and your sister is being bull-headed. Like you were once upon a time," she reminded me.

"We not talking about me."

"Uh huh. Why did you bring the girl to live here? It's not about your rental business you run through your condos in the city."

"Just feel like she needs to be close... I can't explain it."

"Hmm. Well, I can feel she's a good person. The girl damn near wanted to break down in front of me but held it together. She'll be fine here."

"Good, because I have to leave in a few days for California. I'm going to be opening a dispensary out there."

"Work, work, work and some more work," she mocked me as I kissed her on the cheek.

"Money makes the world go around, crazy woman." She smiled and balled her fist up at me.

"I have to go to the tanning shop and speak to the contractor. Renovations should be done next week."

"And what about the staff?"

"I got it handled."

"You need an assistant, Yoshon. Stop trying to do everything by yourself. That girl has no business working at the tanning salon; you need to hire her as an assistant. Let her pick through applications and help you with your other businesses. Give her a chance."

What my grandmother was saying wasn't a bad idea. I could use someone who looked over my businesses and helped me out. As of now, I was the one doing all of it on my own, and the shit had me stressing the fuck out. If I hired help, it would be easier to manage shit. Still, I liked to do shit myself, and that was an issue when you had employees. You needed to delegate, and it was something that I had to learn.

"I hear you." She lowered her eyes and pursed her lips because she knew I was full of shit. It didn't hurt to pretend to act like I was going to listen to her suggestion.

Heading upstairs, I went into my room and called Eva. For the past two days she had been blowing my phone up, and I've been ignoring her. She answered soon as the call connected.

"Hey," was all she said. I could tell from her dry tone that she was pissed that I had been ducking her phone calls.

"What's good? I've been busy with shit, so I couldn't get back to you."

"So busy that you couldn't shoot me a text message? Yoshon, I'm trying, and I don't feel like you're giving me the same energy back. Let me know if I'm wasting my time because I got other people waiting to date me."

"Stop playing with me before I lay you over my knee and spank ya ass," I threatened, and she giggled. I knew I could get her to crack a smile.

"Don't try and butter me up, Yoshon. I miss seeing your face, why aren't you making that happen?"

"Let me take you out to dinner tonight. I'll come pick you up around nine."

"Hmm, that's last minute, so I need to check my calendar, you know I'm busy," she teased. Eva knew she wanted to scream yes soon as I offered dinner.

"I guess I can ju—"

"Don't play with me," she giggled. "I'll be ready, and you better be on time," she demanded.

"Bet. See you later tonight, Beautiful."

"Wait one second, how's Pit Pat?"

"She's good, you know she asks about you."

"Then stop keeping me away," she made sure to add.

"I'll see you tonight, Eva."

After I ended the call, I pulled something out for tonight and showered before changing. I had a lot of driving ahead of me. Tonight, I planned to get some sleep in my bed, but if I ignored Eva another night, she wouldn't hesitate to pop up and check on me.

WE WERE HALFWAY through dinner and Eva kept rubbing her feet on my leg. I knew she wanted to leave and head to her crib. If it was any other night, I would have taken her home and beat her guts out her body. Tonight, Pit Pat made me promise that I would make it back in time for dinner. Because I knew I had the date with Eva and couldn't cancel, I made her meet me for seven instead of nine tonight. She complained about the time, still, her ass made sure she was ready when I pulled up to her crib. Pit Pat was making Ox tails, potato salad and rice and beans. I ordered some steak and mash potatoes that I pretended I didn't like just to save room for Pit Pat's good. Eva could tell something was off and I could see she was trying to avoid bringing it up by trying to turn up the sexual energy.

Hey, I'm here! Where are you? I stared at the text message from Hazel. I knew she wanted to pick my brain about something with my sister. Part of me was happy to be here so I could avoid the conversation altogether.

"I'll take the check," I told the waiter, when he came to refill our champagne flute.

"No dessert, Sir?"

See, this is the shit I couldn't stand. Nigga, I asked for the check which meant I didn't want dessert. Here he go suggesting something I didn't want. He must of understood my facial expression because he quickly fixed his last statement. "Let me go ahead and retrieve your check."

"Yeah. Go and do that," I told him and he scurried away.

Eva was staring at me and I knew she was about to start her shit too. She didn't like when our dates were being rushed. It happened one other time because I had to rush out of town, and she stopped talking to me for two weeks. If I could, I would have stayed with her all night at her apartment. Except, when I made a promise to my grandmother, I always came through for her, no matter what.

"Why do I feel like you're rushing to get out of here?"

"I just got a lot of stuff to do in the morning and need to get some sleep. I've been running on close to nothing this past few days, feel me?" It wasn't a lie. I did have shit that I needed to handle tomorrow, and these past few days had been a blur.

"Hmmm, so why don't I just stay at your place tonight? You probably have to head back to the city in the morning anyway."

I did, but she didn't need to know that. "Nah, I'm actually heading toward Delaware." When the words left my mouth, she examined me closely, as if she was trying to stare the lie out of me.

"I'm off tomorrow. I'll ride along with you."

Screwing my face up, I stared at her, and she looked away because she knew she had just played herself. "When have I ever handled business around you?"

"Maybe you should. Six months, Yoshon? Where are we going with this? It's been six months and I feel I'm nowhere close to a commitment from you." She continued to sulk.

"Why does everything have to move on your time? How you

know six months is long enough for me to give the kind of commitment you want?"

"Six months is a decent time with everybody. Usually, I would have been your girlfriend by now. Instead, I'm a booty call, who you take out on dinners."

"Yo, you really fronting right now." Eva tried to act like all I did was take her out to dinners. I remember us doing museums, movies, and shopping together. Shit, she spent a few days over my crib with me and we chilled the entire time and ate food.

"It's fine, Yoshon. I'll find my own way home," she gathered her things and attempted to get up. She made eye contact with me, read my expression and placed her purse back on the table. "What? I wanna leave."

"Act a fool in here and I'll show you how it's done," was all I said to her.

Where did I go wrong with women? Eva was twenty-eight and had her shit together, so I didn't want to put her in the young category. Yet, some of her actions proved otherwise. She could be a brat when she wanted to. The waiter brought the check, and I paid with cash; I was so pissed with her. A nigga didn't even want to wait for him to slide my credit card and shit, I needed to bounce now. Holding hands, we exited the restaurant and got to the valet, who was already waiting with our car doors opened. I held Eva's door opened and watched as she slid into the seat and then tipped the valet driver.

"Can you hurry and take me home?"

"Keep acting the fuck up and I'll drop you at the train station. Eva, you already know I don't do the petty shit, and I'm not going to cater to your baby ass attitude. I don't have no kids, and I damn sure like to think that I'm not dating one."

"I'm just frustrated."

"So, speak on that shit like a grown ass woman. I don't like baby footing and all these immature games; I'm a grown man, Eva."

"So, act like a fucking man, Yoshon!" she screamed and then leaned back to cross her arms.

"Yeah, I'm gonna drop your ass off until you can act like the fucking lady I met six months ago. I been trying to ignore your little attitudes and shit, but yeah, you 'bout to get the same treatment back." Pressing my Ferragamo loafer on the gas a little harder, I zoomed down the block toward her apartment. Eva didn't live too far from the restaurant, which is why I opted to take her here instead. She wanted to go somewhere on City Island, and a nigga wasn't about to do all that driving.

From the corner of my eye, I could see tears coming down her cheek as she continued to sit there with her arms folded. Yeah, I understood we hadn't been spending a lot of time together, and it was because I had businesses to run, and she worked fulltime. Then, she kept pushing this commitment shit on me hard. Something in me wouldn't allow me to take that step with her. Each time I thought I was ready for it, it never happened. Pit Pat loved her and that's all that mattered. Yeah, I was feeling her and could see myself getting married and raising a family with her, still, I stalled when it came to telling her I wanted her to be my girl. If that wasn't enough, I had to hear her complain about how she's tired of being a booty call or a friend with benefits. The shit was a headache.

"Don't worry about waiting around," she snapped as she grabbed her purse and hopped out the whip before I could fully put it into park. I watched as she strutted in her navy-blue form-fitting dress up the stairs in front of her building.

Valentine's day was only a few weeks away. She was upset now, but she would conveniently get over it by the time it was time to get some gift, flowers, and candy on massacre day. I watched until she got into the building safely and pulled off. She pissed me off because she knew I hated when she touched the door handle and got out without me holding the door for her. Eva could sit and have her own damn pit party. She was hollering about me not spending no time, but when my ass was sending her Chanel bags with roses for no reason at all, she wasn't complaining. Or, when I picked her up and took her to five-star restaurants for lunch, she was mum. The shit pissed me off because I was trying. Jumping into marriage just because I wanted a wife was something I refused to do. The shit had to happen organically, or I wasn't with the shit. Ten years down the line, I didn't want to look at my wife and think that I only married her because she kept pushing the subject. Settling wasn't something I ever did, and I didn't plan on doing the shit now.

When I pulled up to my crib, I spotted Hazel's car. Staring at my clock, I made it in time for dinner. Walking into the house, I sat my take out on the foyer table and made my way to the kitchen. Pit Pat was plating the food on the Versace glass. It was the glass she used during holidays, so I knew if I missed this, she was going to be pissed with me. When she noticed me, she smiled.

"You have never broken a promise yet," she said her famous line whenever I came through for her.

"And I don't plan to," I took my suit jacket off and placed on the back of the stool. "Where's everyone?"

"In the dining area. Go on and sit, I'm coming and don't need no help." She forced me out the kitchen. Walking down the hall, I entered the dining room, and everyone was seated.

Golden had her hair straightened with a face full of make-up. Shorty was beautiful before, but right now, she was doing something to me. Hazel was sitting across from Golden having a good conversation because they didn't notice I was in the room until Gyan spoke up.

"Hey, Mr. Yoshon," he stood up and came over to give me a dap. "The food smells good, right? Your house is huge," he said all of this in one breath. Little homie was cool as hell. The entire ride back to the crib from his school, he questioned me on a bunch of shit.

"Yeah, Pit Pat knows how to throw down in the kitchen. You in for some good Belizean food tonight. You ever been or heard of Belize?"

"No."

"It's where my grandmother is from. She cooks the best food from there," I informed him and then took a seat next to him and Golden. "You look beautiful."

She blushed. "It's been a long time since I've been called that. Pit Pat insisted that I put on some makeup and get dressed."

"She called me and told me the same thing," Hazel chimed in. I stared at her confused because Hazel rarely went out without looking like she was a hustler's wife. Everything had to be perfect when she stepped out the crib. So, I knew Pit Pat didn't call her ass and tell her anything.

"Well, you look fine as f... beautiful," I caught my words before I cursed in front of this boy.

"Thank you, Yoshon. Did your business meeting go well?"

"Yeah, it went as expected. Business is business. Did you show Gyan his room and sh.. stuff?" Eva had me so pissed the fuck off that I couldn't stop cursing. It was hard to turn the shit off when I was pissed already. The way she showed her ass tonight had me ready to delete her damn number and change my fucking bank.

"Glad everything worked out for you." She took a sip of champagne.

"I see you got acquainted with my big head sis in law."

"Ugh, you tried it. I was telling her to come to the salon and let me hook her up," Hazel replied.

"My sister would have been here, but she probably handling business and couldn't make it." I didn't bother to call Yolani because I knew she wouldn't come, or she would come late and pissed Pit Pat off.

"Yeah, you know how business comes first for her. I haven't seen her since the other day. We're like two ships passing in the night," Hazel went on to spill her marital issues to us.

"Word." What else she wanted me to say?

"Business comes first in your marriage? I've been in a relationship like that, and it's not fun," Golden told her.

"It's not fun. We're w—"

"Okay, dinner is served," Pit Pat announced as she had the only housekeeper she trusted to bring out our food.

Rolanda worked twice a week, and those were the days that Pit Pat went over to Yolani's house to make sure things were together with her house. Usually, she would stay the night after cleaning her entire house, doing laundry and cooking. Telling our grandmother, she didn't have to care for us was like telling her we didn't need her fucking help, so we didn't. I understood that this was what made her happy, so I allowed her to do what made her happy. She spent so many years sacrificing to raise us, that whatever made her happy was what I allowed her to do.

"Rolanda, I know you're staying for dinner?"

She smiled and shook her head. "Ms. Santana has tried to convince me to stay. I have to get home to my babies and get them ready for school tomorrow. Enjoy, and set me a plate to the side." She placed all the dishes down on the table.

"Alright, we'll put a plate to the side for you." I winked, and she headed out of the dining room. Pit Pat sat down at the head of the table and smiled at all of us.

"We're just missing my Lani. You will bring her a plate home, okay?" She stared at Hazel and she nodded her head.

We all said grace and then started fixing our own plates. All that could be heard was the sound of the silver against the glass plates and bowls. Golden fixed Gyan a plate and then stared at me.

"Sit, I'll fix you one," she demanded and leaned over the table to fix the food onto my plate. I couldn't front like my eyes didn't land on her ass in that dress she wore. The shit was sitting up and her waist looked as if she didn't give birth to this boy sitting beside me.

"Pit Pat, one second and I'll fix yours too. It's only right since you prepared all of this food," she told Pit Pat and smiled.

Pit Pat was one for arguing about how much she could for herself, but this time, she remained quiet and allowed her to fix my plate and then fix hers too. "Well, shit, you can go ahead and add some oxtail gravy on my white rice," Hazel joked.

Golden reached across and placed the gravy over her rice. "It's the least I could for all of you. You both opened your home to me, and for that, I'm forever grateful," she spoke as she sat down.

"Thank you, Golden. I appreciate it." Pit Pat smiled and held her wine glass up. We all held our glasses up and did a quick toast before eating our food.

Pit Pat spoke about everything under the sun and Golden ate it up. Me and Hazel heard the stories a million times. Even Gyan chimed in a few times to ask if she was really raised around goats and sheep. I continued to eat and kept stealing glances at Golden as she ate and engaged in conversation with my grandmother. It was something about this woman. Her beauty, her poise, and conversation intrigued me. Even in her current predicament, she didn't carry herself like less than. Still, she stood with her poise and head held high as she engaged in conversation. If I was a guest, I would have never assumed this woman was sleeping her car two days ago. Her name fit, because her essence was Golden.

After dinner, I kissed and hugged Hazel and told her to let me know when she made it home. Then, I headed to my office. With the door opened, I could hear Pit Pat and Golden still talking like old buddies. I logged onto my computer and checked sales reports and shit like that. Then I went to search for old abandoned properties that were foreclosed on. Flipping houses was something I always wanted to get into. With my hands in so much shit, I don't know what was holding me back. With all the money I had, there was no need to push drugs or guns. The reason I kept it around was because of Yolani. This life wasn't for her; she couldn't be in suits and holding business meetings. She wanted to be in the streets and getting it the illegal way. College was what I wanted for my baby sis, yet she had other plans. Yolani wanted to be a bully in the streets, which she was. She wanted people to fear her and it was more about the fear than the money. Seeing my mom's get bodied in her bedroom, really fucked her up.

"Good night, baby," Pit Pat came around the desk and kissed me on the forehead. "That Golden is a beautiful, but pained woman." She hugged me.

"I heard you both chopping it up in there. Everything put up?"

"No, she made me go upstairs and rest. These old feet are swelling." She pulled her skirt up to reveal her feet.

"Yeah, the party is done for you. Go on and get some rest. Tomorrow, you don't need to get up for breakfast."

"Yosh—"

"No! I have one Pit Pat, and I can have a million Johnny cakes, anytime. But, I can't have a million you."

She did her favorite expression and pursed her lips before kissing me on my forehead again and carried herself upstairs. I knew she wouldn't listen, but it felt nice to tell her what to do for once. It felt like it had been ten minutes since Pit Pat headed upstairs, but it had really been two hours. Shutting down my computers, I heard glasses clink in the kitchen and went to investigate. When I rounded the corner, Golden was sitting at the counter enjoying a glass of wine. Her eyes were closed as she enjoyed every sip. When her eyes opened, they landed on me, and she removed the glass from her lips.

"I probably look foolish, huh? I haven't had a good wine in months. The only relief I get is a cheap beer," she giggled. "Want a glass?"

Nodding my head, I walked around the island, leaned back and watched as she moved around my kitchen like she had been doing so for years. She located a glass and poured me a glass and returned to her seat.

"How did you enjoy dinner?"

"It was delicious. It was all Gyan spoke about before bed. We're so appreciative of you and your grandmother." She made sure to mention.

"You serving us during dinner didn't prove that?" I snickered, and she flipped her middle finger at me. "There she is."

"Who?"

"The smart ass. You polish up around my grandmother, huh?"

"I have respect." She took a sip of her wine.

"Oh, is that what you call that? Would you like anything, Pit Pat?" I mocked her and she rolled her eyes at me.

"So, you're going to clown because I have respect? What about you, Dapper Dan? You're dressed way dressy than I remember meeting you two days ago."

"Can't be dressed down all the time, right?"

"I guess." She poured more wine into her glass and savored the taste. "How did your date go?"

"Date?" How the fuck did she know?

"Pit Pat told me about your girlfriend."

"She's a friend, not my girlfriend."

"Does she know that?"

"Wouldn't be here tonight if she didn't."

"Well, like I told Pit Pat, I just want to do what I have to do so I can provide for my son. I don't want her to get upset with me or think this is anything more than you helping me out."

"You're good. About providing for your son. I've been needing an assistant for a minute. What you think of helping me out?"

"Oh, so you don't need me at the tanning salon? I'm a little offended," she laughed.

"Nah, I need you to skim through applications to hire the staff there. The pay is well, and I'm sure you'll be able to afford something in a few months."

Looking around the kitchen, she smiled. "Well, it's not like I'm staying at a shelter for the time being."

"Right."

"I accept the job and when can I start?"

"Now. I need some ice."

"Yeah, alright. I'm about to go to sleep and get up so I can beat Pit Pat in this kitchen. You see her feet? She shouldn't be cooking nothing."

"She hard headed. Tomorrow, you can drop Gyan off to school in the BMW."

Her eyes widened, and she looked at me as if I lost my mind. "Seriously?"

"Yeah, I need you to stop in the city at Saks to pick me up a suit my personal shopper pulled for me. Find some matching shoes too. Starbucks when you return too. Chai latte."

"Noted. Have a good night, Mr. Santana." She smiled and headed upstairs. Her ass switched back and forth as she headed out the kitchen and I enjoyed the view.

Guzzling two more cups of wine, I headed upstairs to shower and relax before morning came. I had a funeral to attend for one of my street soldiers. He was sixteen and had his entire life ahead of him. Yolani fought me tooth and nail to allow him to sell work for her. This was the nasty side of the business that people didn't see. Paying for the funeral and paying my respect was the least I could do for the family. After showering, I climbed in bed, closed my eyes and tried to get some rest. That beauty down the hall made it damn near impossible to do so.

10

Hazel

"DAMN, feel like I haven't seen you in mad long." Yolani dragged herself into our kitchen at eight in the morning. I could smell the weed and liquor before she passed doorway of the kitchen. From the way she swaggered in, I could tell she still had some in her system, and the way she dragged her words, I knew she was feeling nice.

"You haven't," my response was short and blunt. There was no need for me to sugarcoat anything. My wife hadn't seen me in a few days, and it bothered me. Instead of her being home or knowing my whereabouts, she was worried about drinking and getting high with her workers. It irritated me that she was standing in front of me with glossy eyes and a silly grin fixed on her face.

"Damn, I come home and get attitude. I came home the other night, and you weren't here... all night," she added.

My heart stopped because I spent the entire night with

Denim. I prayed God forgive me for sleeping with someone outside of our marriage. Denim was just... Denim and I wanted it. I wanted to feel wanted and caressed. I wanted someone to whisper sweet nothings in my ear or lay in bed in the afterglow of passionate sex. He gave me all the things I wanted from my wife, the woman I married. The fact that I didn't return home didn't encourage her to worry about where I could have been. Instead, she went back out and did what she was great at; running the streets.

"Went to hang out with Mo and ended up staying over and helping her with the kids." My best friend, Mo was my quick recovery. If Yolani called, she would lie without me needing to fill her in beforehand.

"Oh, word? Thought you both were taking a break now that she has a new nigga." She went into the fridge and grabbed a bottle of water. She stopped when she seen a plastic container in the fridge. "You went by Pit Pat's?"

"Yes. She invited me over for dinner. I called you and your phone went to voicemail. Your brother is helping a friend out and she's staying there with them along with her son."

"Friend? He doesn't let people we've grew up with stay the night... who is he?"

"Um, I just said *she* has a son, Yolani. Why are you all like this? Something isn't right with you." I walked closer to her and she backed up from me.

"Why you trying to be in my shit? I'm tired and been out in the streets, let a nigga take a breather before breathing down my neck!" she barked before heading upstairs.

Shaking my head, I continued to sit at the island while checking my social media messages. It bothered me that me and Yolani was at this place in our relationship. Then again, it didn't surprise me. This was the regular routine and it was something I had to learn to get used to. While I was heading out to head to the shop, she was coming in to sleep the day away. Then, when I came home, she was heading out. We had no time for us to spend time or reconnect after working. I understood that she had to work, and bills had to get paid. Still, where did I fit in to all of that?

Coming to take you to lunch today. Make sure you don't book no appointments, Denim's message popped up on my phone.

Looking behind me, a smirk came on my face thinking of the way he stroked my kitty. Even when I got up the next morning and tried to do the walk of shame out of his hotel room, he stopped me and made me cuddle with him until noon. When I awoke from our nap, he had lunch spread out in the sitting room, and we enjoyed each other's company. It was beautiful or is that too corny. The simple things are what made me revisit the moment a million times in my head.

"Don't forget to put the security code on. You be forgetting that shit all the time," Yolani made sure to yell down the stairs before she closed our bedroom door.

Lunch sounds good. See you then. Each time she pissed me off, it just made me want to be with Denim that much more. Maybe God was telling me something and I wasn't listening to him.

Tossing my unfinished drink into the sink, I grabbed my keys along with my purse and headed out the house, purposing forgetting to put on the security code. Yolani was going to learn that I wasn't one of her workers and she couldn't just talk to me anyway and think I was going to accept it.

When I arrived at the shop, everyone was setting up while six people waited to be seen. After I greeted everyone, I headed to my office and my best friend, Mo, followed right behind me. I knew she was being nosey because I hadn't been in the shop for the past few days.

"Where have you been, 'cause you sure haven't been here?" She smacked her tongue and sat in the seat in front of me.

"Taking much needed time off." Mo could tell something was off and she just in the seat in front of my desk and observed me.

"You got some dick... only dick will have you whistling while shuffling through all those bills," she called out.

"Um, what? You know I'm married to Yolani, so how is that possible?"

"That plastic dick don't have you humming and going through those bills. Spill it," she demanded and crossed her legs as she got comfortable.

"Denim is back," was all I had to say for her eyes to pop out of her head. "Mo, you don't need t—"

"Denim that wanted to marry you? Denim that was ready to whisk you away to the west coast and make you his wife?"

"Yes, Denim is just fine to use. Not too many people walking around with the name Denim."

"How the fuck did that happen?" she questioned.

"He's back in town and says he's back for me. But, that's a lie. He's opening a store here and wanted to catch up."

"How did catching up end up with your legs opened?"

"Who said they were opened?"

"That smile on your face. Hazel, what the hell?"

Mo was shocked because this wasn't me. I wasn't the one who slept around, especially with old flings. I was the committed housewife who ran her business and catered to her wife. Who was this person emerging from inside of me? Not only did I cheat on Yolani, I was ready, willing and prepared to do it again.

Falling into my chair, I put my head back. "He makes me smile. It's like no time past by us when we connected. Things haven't been the best with me and Yolani."

"Hmph, I heard."

"What do you mean you heard?"

"Hazel, do you think the streets are silent? Yolani is out here living life like she doesn't have a ring on her finger, and you at home. I'm sorry you're hearing it from me, but you need to check your wife. And, messing around with Denim isn't good either.

This man wants you, and if you can't give yourself to him fully, you need to stop leading him on."

This was one of the main reasons I hated having heart to hearts with Mo. She was always right and would tell you about yourself. You couldn't argue because what she spoke was pure facts. You could argue with opinions all day, but when it came to facts, you couldn't argue with that. Crazy thing is that Denim told me what he wanted upfront. He didn't hide the fact that he wanted me... he wanted us. I chose to ignore it while having my fun with him. It was wrong, but who was I kidding? Leaving Yolani would be a nightmare. She would never sign divorce papers and she would make my life a living hell.

"I hear you," I sighed. "Anyway, how's the kids? Chikae still modeling?"

"Yeah, she just got booked for some store in the city. It's a city-wide campaign, so my baby's face will be all over the city."

"Aye, go diva! And you? What about school?"

"You already know I'm still going to class. The goal is to finish, and I can't let my three babies down," she smiled.

Mo was a single mother, and she never let that shit get her down. If her kids needed something, she would move hell and high water to make sure they had everything and then some. She owned her own home, car and went to school at nights while the kids slept. During the day, she worked at the receptionist here and always made it home to prepare a hot meal for them. When I thought of mom goals, she was the definition of it.

"Good. Do I have any bookings today?"

"Yep, five."

"Can you move them away from lunch? I want to take lunch today." When I requested her to remove my appointments from lunch, her eyes narrowed in on me, and she stared at me until I finally broke and told her.

"Denim wants to take me to lunch. What?"

"I told you that you're messing with fire, Hazel. That man

wants you, and you know it, but want to keep playing games. You can't play tit for tat with Yolani, with this man's heart."

"I hear you, Mo. All I'm trying to do is have lunch and reconnect with a friend. Why is it so wrong for me to go out and enjoy someone else's company, but Yolani is free to do whatever she wants?"

"Because I know that's not what you're about. If Yolani was doing everything she was supposed to, you wouldn't be worried about Denim. He could have called you and you would have had his number blocked the next time he tried to call you. Two wrongs don't make a right."

"They don't? I could of sworn they did." Mo rolled her eyes and stood up with her hand on her hip.

"I'm not going to deal with you today. I got actual work that needs to be done, and you playing around. I'll move your appointments around, so you can go to your little lunch."

"That's all I ask. Thank you!" I smirked as she closed the door behind me.

Two wrongs didn't make a right and I completely understood that. Still, while Yolani was out doing what she wanted, I was the only one in our marriage. It was a lonely feeling when the person you were supposed to be with, played you off to go run the streets. The infidelity wasn't something I witnessed with my own eyes. The rumors were enough for me to accuse her and when I did she would get upset and yell about how I stay listening to bitches. Any bitch that decided to come to me as a woman, was going to have me come to them like a doctor, 'cause they were going to be a patient in somebody's hospital. It was bad enough that I had tried to calm down from my craziness. Yoshon had to continue to tell me that every situation didn't need a reaction from me, and he was right. Bitches wanted to be in my place and would kill to be Yolani's wife. They saw the cars, house, nail shop and the fact that I had any and everything that came out, and they wanted it. If only they were able to see the lonely nights, miscommunication, verbal disrespect and the constant begging I did to be a priority in Yolani's wife. If they saw all of that, the designer shoes and foreign cars wouldn't be all that appealing then.

"WHAT ARE YOU DOING HERE?" I gasped when Denim walked through the doors of YoYo's. He smiled and came over and wrapped me in a huge hug.

His hugs were everything and the way he swooped me up and then kissed the crook of my neck made me want to melt into his arms. "You dubbed my call for lunch, so I'm gonna take you out for dinner tonight."

"Dinner? You know what happened last time we had dinner," I pulled him into my office as I whispered.

We had a few people getting their nails finished that were staring and whispering. I didn't need everybody in my damn business. "We were super busy today. I tried to move some appointments around, but they weren't having it today. Business comes first," I explained.

He walked up to me and stood in front of me, blocking any chance of me slipping away from him. Sitting on the edge of my desk, I stared up into his eyes. Everything that Mo had said to me ran through my mind. Denim wasn't playing, and he wanted this.

"I know what happened last time, and I want it to keep happening. You got plans or something?" He snuck a kiss on my lips and I allowed him to. It felt so good to be loved on and feel wanted. I just wanted to soak all his attention up and bottle it up for later.

"I didn't have any plans as of yet. The night is still young."

"Nah, you had plans now. You know the hotel I'm staying in." He pecked me on the lips and then headed out of my office.

"What if I—"

"Not trying to hear none of that today. Go home and handle

whatever you gotta do with your wifey, and then I'll see you at my hotel room." I wanted to ask why we were going to a hotel when he had a condo we could go to. Instead, I kept my mouth shut and smiled as he closed the door behind him.

Thankfully, Mo had left for the day. If she was here, she would have had a mouth full, and I didn't need that right now. The devil was talking to me on my shoulder and he was telling me to do what I wanted. The angel on my shoulder was somewhere tied up with tape because she wasn't speaking to me, and I didn't need her input right about now. When I came out of my office, the two nail techs were finishing up their clients. Eisha was sitting at her station on the phone. It didn't matter how early or late I needed her to be here; she would be here. Along with being talented with her skill, she was also loyal and just wanted to do her work and go home at the end of the day. Unlike other shops, there weren't drama between my girls. They all got along, kept personal business out the shop and did what they had to do.

"I'm gone... lock up the shop when these ladies are done," I told her and passed the shop's keys to her. "I know you have two early clients, so you'll need to open too."

"Thanks, Haze. See you tomorrow." She smiled and then continued with her conversation. Since I owned the shop, I was able to park right out front. Sliding into my car, I started the engine and headed toward home. All I wanted was a shower and then a second to think about if I was going to take Denim up on his offer.

Soon as I walked through the door, I was annoyed. Yolani's shoes were all over the foyer and I could spot three pairs of pants laid out on the stairs. She always complained that we needed to bring the huge mirror in our living room, upstairs, so she would get dress downstairs, so she could stare at herself in the mirror. Sighing, I kicked her shoes to the side and made my way into the kitchen where I heard her on the phone – as always. When she saw me, she gave me a simple head nod. A head nod like I was another one of her workers in the streets, not her wife. This was how my wife greeted me after not seeing or hearing from me all day.

"What's all of this? You're gonna clean all of this up, right?" she waved at me to shut my mouth and the continued conducting business. Looking around, I know she didn't shush me in my own damn house. "Have you fucking lost your mind?"

Her eyes widened, and she huffed as she rushed off the phone. "Why the fuck you gotta come in here yelling and shit? I've been trying to hook up with this nigga and his team for months. He finally had time to chat and you come in being loud as fuck while popping those damn gums!" she hollered at me.

"I don't give a damn about who you've been trying to fucking hook up with. You got my house with your shoes and clothes all over the damn place. Then, you got dishes in the sink with the ketchup sitting out on the counter with dried ketchup around it. If that isn't the worst of it, you gonna nod your head like I'm some nigga in the streets!" I slammed my hands down on the counter as she stared blankly at me.

It was a look she always gave me, and I couldn't place my finger on it. She always seemed to be spaced out and not paying attention to me. It was as if her body was in front of me, but her soul was elsewhere. Snapping out of it, she sniffled and went into the fridge, ignoring everything I said.

"I'm out. You always trying to bitch about something. When the fuck do I come home to something cooked and my wife not nagging? The fuck."

"You deadass right now? Yolani Santana, you don't ever come the fuck home for me to do any of that. Like now, you're leaving." She tried to walk past me, and I shoved her. I watched her stumble back a few inches and then suck her teeth. "No!" I screamed.

"You deadass, Haze?" Stop acting like a little ass girl." She shoved me hard. I stumbled back and regained my balance and ran to the front door.

"You're not leaving until you talk to me! Leaving every time we argue isn't going to solve anything!" I hollered.

Tears were forming, and I was upset. Marriages weren't easy and they took time, still, people made it work. Yolani made time for shit she wanted to do, and I or our marriage wasn't what she wanted to do.

"Move the fuck out my face before I punch you in your shit!" she sneered and yanked me away from the door and tossed me onto the floor.

Her actions had me so stunned that I didn't move from under the foyer table. I sat there shocked that she had handled me that way and then continued to walk out the door, not bothering to check on me. Instead, I was met with the loud slam of our front door. A few seconds later, I heard her screech out of our driveway. Breaking down, I pulled my legs close to my chest and sobbed. How did things get so bad? Why didn't she want to work on this like I did? If she didn't make it clear before, Yolani made it crystal clear that she didn't want to have anything to do with me or our marriage. The pain of being rejected by someone you loved hurt physically. People didn't understand the pain of heartbreak. It felt like someone was gripping your heart so tight that you couldn't eat, sleep or think without wanting to break down. My chest felt tight and I felt like I was going to pass out.

Picking myself up on the floor, I grabbed my purse and keys from the counter in the kitchen and locked up behind myself. With tears streaming down my eyes and snot coming out my nose, I dialed Denim's number and he answered almost immediately.

"Can I see you?" I sobbed into the phone.

"Yo, what's wrong with you?"

"I just need to see you," I wailed as I tossed my purse into my car and slammed the door after I got in.

"Yeah, come to my crib. I'm texting you the address now. Hurry up too," he told me and we ended the call.

Making the drive to Denim's house was long and painful. Being in the car with my thoughts drove me up the wall. How could she do me like I was nothing? Yolani acted as if she didn't know me and I was some stranger she was pushing around. My blood boiled, my heart ached, and my feelings were all over the place. Why me? Why us? My parents tried to warn me that just because we were good friends didn't mean we would be good in a relationship. When the words left my mother's mouth, I knew she was hating. Me and Yolani completed each other's sentences, how wouldn't we work in a relationship. The saying a hard head makes a soft ass was ringing true right about now.

When I made it to Denim's condo, he was waiting downstairs for me. I parked in the guest parking spot and he whisked me upstairs. Snot and tears invaded my face as people in the building stared at me, confused. If they only knew, I felt like my entire life had just ended and couldn't be fixed. Yolani was tough and she rarely showed emotion. It was part of the reason I fell for her. As a friend, I was able to always break down that wall and get her to reveal her feelings to me. When we got into a relationship, it's like she worked double time to keep that wall up and prevent from me tearing it down. I understood she had been through a lot and some stuff wasn't as easy to get over, but to push me out the way she did, hurt me to my core.

"What happened? She put her hands on you?" Denim questioned as he held my arms and bent down to stare me in the eyes.

"No," I lied. She did put her hands on me when she tossed me onto the floor like a rag doll. Denim didn't know that much, so I kept it to myself. My feelings were more hurt than my knees and hands when I hit the floor.

"Ma, come on, so I can get you some tissue. What happened that she got you out here with snot and shit all over your face?

This isn't the Hazel that I know." He lifted me up and sat on his kitchen counter.

"The Hazel you knew was overrated," I mumbled and messed around with my jeans. The Hazel he knew would have took her ass to California and got everything she wanted. She would have been married with that little cute girl he called his daughter as her own.

"Stop," he told me and handed me the wet napkin. "What are you really doing, Haze? Shorty got you crying and shit, for what?"

"I'm married to her, Denim. You don't understand because you're not married. It's more than just up and leaving her."

"Word? So, you want to sit and fix this shit with her? Let me know, because I don't need to be wasting my time. If you gonna choose her again, let me know so I can work on mending my heart now."

"No, it's... it's not what I'm saying, Dem. You're putting everything on me right now and I don't know anything!" I screamed, and tears came down my face. I cried and cried hard.

Denim dropped his shoulders and pulled me to his chest while I cried. "My bad. I don't mean to make this shit hard on you. I apologize, Hazel," he whispered in my ear and kissed me on the ear.

"I just want to be happy." He listened to me sob into his chest.

He pulled me away from his chest and kissed me on the lips. Our tongues danced around in each other's mouth before he broke our kiss. "That's something you have to do. It's not something me or Yolani can give you. Yeah, I know I can make you happy, but that shit starts from you first."

"Fuck me, Dem," I demanded. My mind was all over and all I wanted to do was fuck. I wanted him to pull my hair and spank me from behind.

"Not like this." He kissed me on the lips and left the kitchen.

Jumping down from the counter, I followed him into his bedroom. He had just sat down on his bed, and I jumped between his legs and unbuckled his jeans and belt. Pulling his dick out, it was hard as 11th grade math. My mouth watered at the sight of how pretty his dick was. Bending down, I placed my entire mouth over his dick and made it touch the back of my throat. His grip on my hair let me know I was doing my job right. Gagging, I spit on his dick and shoved it back down my throat with force, and he whimpered. Just because Yolani didn't have a dick didn't mean my head game wasn't something serious. When he was on the verge of cumming, he pulled me up and snatched my jeans down. Bending me over the bed, he shoved all his dick into me with force. Gasping, I leaned over and made my ass clap as he held me tight around my waist.

"Uhh, right there, harder!" I screamed and the more I screamed, the harder he fucked me.

Grabbing a hold of my hair, he pulled my head back. "Tell me how much you want it," he demanded.

"I want it baaaaddddd, baby," I cried out.

The way he was working this curved dick, it was hitting parts of my walls I never knew existed. He pulled out, slapped it on my ass and then slammed it right back inside of me. My lip quivered, the dick was so damn good. Shaking my ass, I pushed it back on him, and he dug his nails into my waist as he pumped harder and harder. When he pulled it out again and slammed it back in, I creamed all over him. Denim was far from done, because he flipped me over and entered me from the front while staring into my eyes.

"You know I still love the shit out of you," he told me and then came. I wrapped my legs around him and planted a kiss on him. We stayed in that position and kissed while being in each other's arms. It felt good to feel wanted and appreciated. When I stared into Denim's eyes, I knew he wanted and loved me. In fact, he never stopped. The last thing I wanted was to break his heart. I was scared to lose love, but even more scared of starting over it again.

11

Yolani

"HOW THE HELL did you get into my apartment?" Cherry questioned as she sat her grocery bags down on the kitchen table. "And why do you have all this coke scattered everywhere?" she continued with that nagging shit that I couldn't stand.

"Instead of you fucking beefing soon as you walk through the door, how about you greet me, bitch?" I responded and continued to sprinkle the coke onto my blunts. My nose was raw as fuck from sniffing, so I was trying to find other ways to get my high. A nigga wasn't about to be smoking no damn crack, so this was the next option besides snorting.

Hazel had me fucked up when she came into the crib from work. She fucked a call for me and then she came in screaming about dumb shit. All she had to do was clean the shit up when I left. Instead she wanna get all fucking childish and put her hands on me. The way I swung her, I didn't mean to do that shit. Hazel knew how to push buttons that weren't meant to be pushed.

When she stood in front of the door, I blacked. All I saw was her laying on the floor when I realized what I did. Yeah, I should have stayed and helped her off the floor. With how mad I was feeling, it was best for me to leave before shit go worst. It wasn't no secret that I had a hand problem, and it was something I promised myself I would never do to Hazel. I would never be able to forgive myself if I laid hands on her.

"What the fuck?" I jumped up when Cherry flipped her entire kitchen table over. The table was glass and shattered soon as it hit the floor.

"I'm tired of you coming when you and your bitch get into a fight. When you're good with her, you don't come the fuck around here. I'm also tired of you fucking coming here to be a fucking junkie. Bitch, go and use a damn trap house, this isn't one of them!" she yelled as she slammed shit around.

Coke was all over the floor along with weed and my roll up. First, Hazel came home with her shit, and I got away from there without putting hands on her, but Cherry was about to catch all the anger I got handed today. Staring at her, she continued to go on and on about what I didn't do for her, and how I was only around when I needed her. There was no lie and she was speaking the truth. Cherry was there when I was going through it with Hazel. It had been a minute since me and Hazel been on the same page, so I frequented her house, handled business from here and acted like it was my second crib. Why go out and get another crib when I could lay up here without having to do much. At first, Cherry was so damn excited to have me in her crib that I got home cooked meals damn near every night. Then, it stopped, and the bitching and moaning came after. She cried about not going out or how I didn't claim her when I saw her out in the hood. Why the fuck would I? She knew when I stepped to her that I was spoken for, and she continued to pursue me. Why did bitches think they could persuade you to leave your woman for them? Bitch, the whole reason I entertained fucking with you is because I needed someone to do my laundry when I went MIA on Hazel. I was trying to have a peaceful space to come and chill, not hear the same shit I could hear at home.

"Damn, crackhead." I heard the tail end of what the fuck she was over there venting about. Call me what the fuck you want, but I wasn't no damn crackhead.

"The fuck you called me?"

"Yolani, stop acting like you're so high and mighty. You fucking running around here with a damn problem. Bet Yoshon don't know his sister is fucking around with the product too, huh?" My brain had communicated with my hand, and it formed a fist. Next thing I knew, I was on top of Cherry, and punching the shit out of her. The bitch was screaming and trying to claw at my face.

Hazel and her bullshit pissed me off, Cherry calling me a crack head added to that, and the fact that I was letting Yoshon down by having this little addiction. I could stop when I wanted, and I wasn't ready to. I was having fun and chilling, right? My hand snagged on something and the pain made me jump back quickly. When I did, Cherry laid there in a pool of her blood and her face was unrecognizable.

"Cherry, stop playing... get up." I kicked her leg. She didn't move and appeared to be dead. Checking her pulse, she barely had life left in her. Grabbing my phone out the glass on the floor, I called Grape.

"Yo?"

"Come to the address I'm 'bout to send to you," that was all I said, and I ended the call. Grape was always in the hood, so I knew he was somewhere close. That nigga didn't retire until the end of the day, and even then, he still never brought his ass to his crib.

Grape arrived twenty minutes later. He told me he was at his favorite Spanish spot that wasn't too far from Cherry's apartment. When he saw everything, his eyes jumped out his socket. Grape was a real reserved dude, not too much made him give a reaction. If he had a reaction, I knew the shit was all bad.

"The fuck happened, Yolani?" he asked as he stepped over the glass and headed over to Cherry. "She alive?"

"Yeah... I mean, when I last checked she was."

He stared at me. "You high?"

"Yeah, I smoked me a L before you came." It was a lie, but he didn't need to know all of that right now. When he needed to know was how the fuck was we going to get her to a hospital?

"What the fuck you want me to do? Call an ambulance for her?"

"What the fuck you mean? I pay you good money to make shit like this disappear," I barked and he stared at me unfazed.

"Your brother pays me, not you. Second, you need to handle this shit on your own. That coke on the floor?"

"Yeah, she was about to roll up her some blunts with some." Why was this nigga focused on the wrong shit?

"Same blunt you were smoking?" He was skeptical.

"Nah, I roll my own blunts. Always will. We got into it because she was stealing shit from me." Cherry wouldn't steal from me. Still, I had to think of a reason why I would beat the shit out of her like this.

"Ight, pull her in the staircase, wipe all this shit down and lock her apartment and call the cops. I'm not getting blood on me, so call your flunkies," he told me and dipped out the apartment. The way he stared at me didn't sit right with me. Grape wasn't going to speak on anything until he had proof. I was safe for now, yet that meant I had to stay on guard around his ass.

Instead of calling my dumb asses, I did all the work alone. I made sure no blood traced back to her apartment. Once I was done, I removed every trace of myself out of her apartment and dipped down the block. Calling the ambulance, I dropped the burner phone into the drain and headed to my crib. Hazel's ass could stop bugging now that I'll be spending a few days away from the streets. When I found out what's good with Cherry, I didn't need to be seen. We had people who could have just killed her and got rid of her body. The thought crossed my mind and it quickly diminished. I couldn't do that shit to Cherry. She got on my nerves and nagged like Hazel, but she didn't deserve to die. I hopped in my whip and headed home with the quickness. My wife was going to be hype to see my ass when I got there. She couldn't stay mad at me, and I knew we would spend all night talking about communicating better. I had a million other ways I'd rather spend my night, but I was going to give her what she wanted.

"Where you at, babe?" I yelled when I walked through the door. The shoes and shit was scattered everywhere.

"Yolani, is that you?" I heard Pit Pat's voice.

"Pit Pat? What you doing here?" She came down the stairs slowly and smiled when she laid eyes on me.

"Why do I have to come to your house to see you?" she embraced me and checked me over like she always did. "You okay, gurl?"

"Yes, Pit. I'm just chilling and getting this money."

"Uh huh, your braids have seen better days," she criticized. "Why your pants so baggy?" s=She nit-picked everything.

"Cause I'm barely eating. Hazel's ass don't never cook and I grab what I can. Where's Hazel?"

"Not here." She stirred something in the pot. I knew she would be the one to get to cooking soon as she stepped through the door of our home. "I was straightening up the bedrooms upstairs before I got down here. She at the shop?"

"Not at ten at night. Pit Pat, you don't need to be up cooking and cleaning?"

"You're right, I shouldn't, but who is going to do it? You? Hazel? I think not." She waved her wooden spoon at me. "Where's your wife at dis time?"

Pulling my phone out, I dialed her number and it went

straight to voicemail. Dialing it again, the same thing happened. "Pit, let me get your phone."

Digging in her apron, she handed me her iphone. I dialed Hazel's number and she answered. "Hey Pit Pat, what's up?"

"Yo, where you at?"

"Oh, you're finally spending time with your grandmother. Nice."

"Kill all that attitude shit and bring your ass home," I demanded and she giggled. The fuck was she giggling at?

"I'm funny now? Don't make me come and drag you wherever the fuck you at!" I barked because I was getting mad. I'm home and she needed to be fucking here with me.

"Yolani, you sound like you need a nap. I'm taking some days for myself, and I'll be home when I feel like it. I'll either see you when I get there, or not. Choice is yours," she snickered and ended the call.

Staring at the call, I was shocked that she fucking ended the call on me. Hazel ran when I said run. If I told her to jump, she was grabbing a ruler and asking me how high I wanted her to jump. The fact that she was out and didn't tell me where she was pissed me off. I took my phone and dialed her best friend's number. Mo answered just as I was about to hang up the phone.

"Yolani, is everything alright?"

"Where's Hazel?"

"In her skin, why?"

"Where the fuck is she? I know you know, what bitch she got whispering in her ear?" This wasn't Hazel. She didn't pull shit like this so somebody had to be in her ear.

"Why does someone have to be in her ear? Maybe she just got tired of your bullshit, did you think of that?"

"I really don't got time for your shit right now. Tell me where my wife is, Mo."

"I don't either. I have a class tomorrow morning and three

babies to get bathed and ready for school. And, I already told you, she's in her skin. Night, Yolani." She ended the call.

Tonight, was play with Yolani night. The shit had me ready to tip this entire house upside down to find out where the fuck she was. Pit Pat held her hand out for her phone and shook her head.

"What now?"

"You do this to yourself. That woman loves you and you push her off as burden. Karma."

"She knew what it was when we got together."

"Hazel knew what it was because she was your best friend, not wife. You being busy as her friend is different than being busy as her wife. Think on that," she told me and headed upstairs.

Sitting on the island, I received a call from Cherry's sister. "Yo," I tried to sound casual and relaxed.

"Oh my God, Yolani. Someone attached Cherry!" she screamed.

"What? How the fuck that happened?"

"The cops are saying someone robbed her for her purse. She didn't have anything in her hands, and then her apartment was in a shamble."

"The cops went into her apartment?"

"No, once the coke on the floor I locked it up and told them she stayed with me. Who could have done this?"

"She dead?"

"They're working on her now. I feel like I can't breathe, you think you can come and wait with me?"

"Nah, I'm out of town right now. I'm about to look for a flight to be there with you. I'm 'bout to pain the town red to find out who did this shit. Stay strong, sis."

"Yolani, she's so lucky to have you. She was telling me she was going to end things with you, and I told her that you were good for her. Thank you!" she cried on the phone. Little did she know, she was crying to the same person who put her in that hospital.

"Don't worry about all of that. Before anything, Cherry is my friend and I'm gonna make sure she's straight. Hold tight and I'll let you know when I can get a flight back home."

"Okay," she sighed and ended the call.

Sitting back, I rubbed my temples and thought about all the shit that had transpired through the day. I was better off staying my ass under the covers and not doing shit. I had my wife pissed at me and now my side bitch was in someone's operating room, fighting for her life. Touching my pocket, I felt the little baggie I hadn't touched since earlier. Grabbing some water, I went upstairs and locked myself in my master suite. If Hazel wasn't coming home, I was about to be in another damn planet until her hardheaded ass decided to bring her ass on home.

12

Golden

PIT PAT HAD WENT over to spend a few days at Yoshon's sister's house. I hadn't met her yet and I didn't want to. From the way Hazel described her wife, I was good not meeting her just yet. It was the weekend and Gyan was downstairs in the basement playing with the million games systems that Yoshon had stored down there. Yoshon had left this morning and told me where the car keys were in case I needed to go somewhere. Pit Pat hadn't had a chance to go food shopping since she cooked, so I took it upon myself to use the cash he had left on the counter for take-out and went food shopping. How much food did he expect us to order? Me and Gyan loved to eat, yet we didn't eat like a family of six, which is how much money he left to feed.

"Mom, I'm done playing the game... is dinner almost finished?" he questioned as he pulled himself up on the stool at the counter.

"I'm just waiting for the cheese and sauce to melt all over.

Look at you, you're sweating," I ran my hand across his forehead. "You okay?"

"Yeah, that game had me upset." He blew it off.

Shaking my head, I chuckled. "Had fun down there? You left me up here all alone." I griped and he laughed at me.

"Mom, can I ask you something?"

"Sure, baby."

"Will Mr. Yoshon get tired us and kick us out like Cindy did?" It hurt my heart that my son had to worry about how long the roof over his head would last. It hurt that he had to witness people letting us down. It was one thing for me to deal with it, but for my son to see it too, hurt like a bitch.

"I'll tell you this. If that ever does happen, mommy will have it set up where we will still have a roof over our heads, okay?"

"Okay," he smiled at me. "Love you, Mom."

"Hmm, I'm not sure how I feel about you calling me mom."

"Mommmmmmm," he dragged his words out.

"Okay, okay, I know, you're growing up. Still hurts though."

I smiled as I went to pull out the stuffed shells I had made for dinner. Along with a salad and freshly baked garlic bread. Cooking had always been my favorite thing to do. Grand could say anything he wanted about me, but he came home every night to a home cooked meal made from scratch. The least I could do was cook and make sure Yoshon had something warm to eat when he made it home. Pit Pat had left me with instructions on how to care for him. I found it funny that she still treated her grandchildren like they needed her help. I guess it kept her busy, so she continued to care for them like she had when they were younger. Gyan licked his lips when he saw me pull the glass pan out of the stove. The cheese was bubbling, and the kitchen was filled with the aromas from the food.

"Go on and set the table so we can eat," I called out to him and he jumped down to go do what I told him to.

Smiling, I stared down at the food because I couldn't wait to eat some of it. I spent all day filling in Pit Pat's house slippers. For the life of me, I didn't know how that woman got around and did as much as she did. After cleaning and trying to settle down to cook, I was exhausted. Still, I would rather take this, than sleeping in my car. Not to mention, no one told me to clean, I just did it on my own. Yoshon wanted me to be his assistant but hadn't provided me with any work yet. The only thing I did was grab a suit for him while taking Gyan to school. Oh, and his coffee. After that, he didn't ask me to do anything else from him. This was my life when I lived with Grand. All I did was care for him and my son, so it was something that I was used to. It still felt strange because I wasn't working two jobs or trying to figure out a way to feed myself and Gyan.

"Okay, it's super-hot." I smiled and placed the plate down in front of my son. The smile on his face was all I needed. He was satisfied and was ready to risk burning himself just to get a quick taste.

"Mama, this is good. I love when you cook," He stuck his fork deeper into his plate.

"You just like to fill your stomach, greedy."

"That too," he chuckled.

We continued to eat and talk about school. He told me about his test he had coming up, and I told him about our plans for the summer. This summer I was going to take my son to Disney world. He had never been and each time I asked Grand, he told me he couldn't get away for a week. I begged and pleaded for us to take a family vacation and it never happened. It bothered me that he could never take time for family. Then again, he was out there living wild and not being faithful to me. If I could go back, I would have followed everything my grandmother told me. She warned me about him and I chose not to listen to her. I chose to listen to this man telling me any and everything, instead of the only woman that was there for me. The woman who raised me when my mother just handed me up and went on about her life.

For years I refused to pick up a phone and check on her because I was angry. She didn't support my marriage, husband and didn't want to be a part of her great-grandchild's life. This whole time I thought I was punishing her, and now that I sit and think about it, I was punishing myself. I was the one who missed out on spending time with my grandmother and absorbing all the wisdom she loved to instill in me.

"Hey... oh, word? You cooked and couldn't fix me a plate at the table?" Yoshon came into the kitchen. He came right on time because I was a few seconds from becoming emotional while thinking of my grandmother.

"Hey, how was your day?" I asked and pointed to the seat next to me. "I'll fix you some right now."

"Nah, I can fi—" he cut his sentence short when he saw the look on my face. He took my advice and sat down. "You gonna stop trying to check me and shit," he laughed.

"Well, if you listened, you wouldn't have to be checked. Now, how was your day?" He watched as I maneuvered around the counter.

"It was good. Had to go and check on a few things. Low-key, I'm happy that I didn't come home to a empty house since Pit Pat's gone," he laughed.

"You lonely or something, Yoshon? To me, you can't be that lonely with that huge hickey on the side of your neck," I pointed out.

He tried to look away and I smiled, letting him know it was cool. It wasn't like I didn't know about his little friend. Pit Pat told me, and I let him know a few nights ago that I knew. He didn't need to hide when he was spending time with her.

"Why you all in my business?" he smirked.

"Not at all. I just see something that wasn't there when you left. It's cool, does she know that I'm here?"

"Why does that matter?"

"It matters because I don't want her to feel like there's something going on between us. I'm a woman and I know how we can get when another woman's around our man."

"Who said she was my woman or that I was her man?"

"That passion mark says otherwise." I sat the plate in front of him and then sat down back in my seat. From his face, I could tell that he was about to demolish this food sitting in front of him.

"Mama, that was so good. Can I go wash up and watch TV in your bedroom?"

"Yes, you can... thank you, baby," I smiled and went to put his plate in the sink. Gyan took off out the room and went to go get ready for bed. We've always slept together since living in Virginia. He didn't like having a separate room from me and neither did I.

"Damn, this bread just melts in your mouth... Pause," he added.

"Thanks. I made it from scratch. Haven't baked bread in close to a year, and I still got it." He nodded his head and tasted the shells.

"Shells is good as fuck too. Who taught you how to cook like this?"

"My grandmother was born in the south. They learned how to cook before walking, and she taught me. Every Sunday she would cook a big meal and it was just the two of us. A few cousins or aunts would always come by for a plate, and it was still too much for just us to eat."

"We might need to make Pit Pat sit down for a few and let you take over the kitchen. Shit good as fuck, and I don't eat everybody food."

"Thanks." I ate some of my salad.

Out the corner of my eye, I could see him staring a hole into my cheek. What was he looking at? Did I have food on my cheek? What the hell was this man staring at. Facing him, I expected him to turn back and act as if he wasn't staring at me, but he didn't. He continued to stare at me.

"You're beautiful. You know that?"

"I've been told plenty of times."

"Did you believe it?" Now, what kind of question was that? Did I believe when someone called me beautiful? When my grandmother called me beautiful, of course, I believed her. When Grand told me, I believed him until his actions showed otherwise. If I was so beautiful, why did you feel the need to cheat with these other women? Why wasn't I enough for you?

"Sometimes I do."

"Do you believe it when I say it to you?" He stared at me. It was as if he was staring into my damn soul with how deep he was staring at me.

"Partly."

"Why partly? Tell me something, who hurt you in your past for you to have this wall up?" Tonight wasn't the night to get all deep about our feelings.

"A lot of people have hurt or let me down. Building this wall up protects me from getting hurt. I have a son depending on me, and I can't keep taking all this heartache and pain every time someone doesn't come through for me or lets me down. I guard myself to stay strong for my son." He watched as I pushed my plate away. My appetite was gone and I didn't want to eat anything anymore.

Yoshon touched my hand gently and I looked up at him. "I got you. If I tell someone I got them; it's because I do. You don't never got to worry about me letting you down, because I got you."

His phone started buzzing on the table and the name Eva popped up. "It's fine. I'm going to clean up in here and watch a movie downstairs," I told him with a smile.

"Nah, I'm talking to you. I'll answer her call later," he told me and held my hand down onto the table. "Do you believe me when I say I got you?"

"Yoshon, I appreciate all that you have done for me and Gyan so far, but I'm just sitting back and waiting for the dream to come to an end."

He looked hurt by my reply. I just met him and didn't expect him to carry me for his entire life. If they people that I've known for years let me down, I didn't expect him, who I've met a few days ago to hold me down.

"Guess I gotta prove that to you," he told me as he ignored the third call. "Let me take this and I'll help you clean the kitchen."

"I got it. Go enjoy your night," I nudged him along.

"We gonna finish this conversation," he told me and got up to take his call. I smiled as I gathered the dishes and went on to cleaning the kitchen. It was the end of the day, and I just wanted to relax and catch up on a movie.

It took me two hours to clean the entire kitchen. Yoshon had went to answer that call and never came back. I assumed he was on the phone smoothing whatever over with his little girlfriend. I carried myself up to my room and found that Gyan went into his own bed. After checking on him, I went to shower. While I washed my hair, I thought about what I wanted in life. Did I want to depend on people for the rest of my life? Yoshon looked as if I hurt his feelings when I doubted what he said. He had to understand that I was used to getting let down. My life had always been a bit of a struggle, and he couldn't expect me to automatically trust what he was saying. His actions were backing up his words now, but what would the future hold? I sauntered out of the bathroom wrapped in a thick pink robe and went into the bedroom.

"Ah, what are you doing in here?!" I screamed and jumped when I saw Yoshon sitting on the edge of the bed.

"I told you we would finish this conversation." He stared at me seriously.

"Boy, if you don't get the hell out this room. That conversation was finished downstairs." I went into my bags on the floor and grabbed some sweats and a shirt.

"Watch a movie with me," he demanded.

"I'm tired... I want to go to sleep."

"And I wanna watch a movie. If you fall asleep, I won't hold it against you."

"Why do you want to watch a movie? Shouldn't you be calling Eva to come and watch a movie with you?"

"Chill. Me and Eva taking a small break right now," he tried to convince me. If he was taking a break because of me, he minds well go on and call whatever little relationship they had, back on.

"Don't take a break because I'm here. I don't plan on being here too long. Since you wanna talk so much, when the hell can I work so I can start making some money?"

"You need to get you a laptop." He smirked. "All I'm trying to do is get to know you better. Is that so wrong?" He touched his chest like he was hurt.

"You're full of it," I laughed. "About this laptop, you providing that?"

"Yeah, if you come and watch a movie with me."

"Negative."

"Yo, you playing games with me like I won't carry your ass out of here and make you watch a movie with me." He stood up and I ran back into the bathroom while giggling. If he picked me up, all my goodies would have been on front street, and he didn't need to see all of that. Quickly, I slid on some panties, sweats and crop top on and came out the bathroom.

"Like I said, you be—" Yoshon came over and swooped me up and carried me out the bedroom. His strong arms held on tight to me as he maneuvered down the stairs into the basement where the projection screen was already set up. I didn't kick or scream because I wanted to watch a movie with him, I just was being difficult.

"All that mouth and your ass let me carry you down here," he said as he placed me gently down on the couch. I watched as he powered down his phone and went over to the bar to fix a drink.

"Golden, you got me feeling some type of way about you," he started.

Pulling my legs under my butt, I stared at him as he fixed the drinks. "Oh yeah? What kind of way are you feeling about me?"

"You don't want to spend no time with me. Got me in my feelings and shit."

"I'm used to spending time with my son or alone. So, don't feel offended, I just like being in my own company."

"Clearly. We living under the same roof, shouldn't we be doing shit together?"

He handed me a light pink drink and sat down beside me. I watched as he kicked his shoes off and kicked them up in the ottoman. "Yum, how did you learn how to make drinks?" I continued to sip this drink.

"Shit, I don't. All I did was mix a bunch of shit in the cup until it stopped looking like a doo-doo green. "

"Oh, how nice."

"I drink my shit straight, but I know you ladies like all that fruity shit. You like it so that's all that matters."

"That I do. Now, how you gonna make it again when you don't know what you did? I like it and I'm gonna want another cup."

"Nah, I don't need you trying to push up on me and shit. Pick a movie," he told me. I went to Netflix and found my favorite movie.

27 dresses was my favorite movie when I was about to get married. I watched that movie over and over again, and it never got old to me. It had been a while since I last watched it and tonight with my drink was a perfect night.

"You would pick a chick flick, wouldn't you?"

"You're going to like it. It's a bomb movie, I promise." He took his drink to his head and then leaned back on the chair. I sipped my drink and got excited for the movie to start.

"I'm bored already. The fuck shorty going to all these weddings for?"

"She's a wedding planner, Yoshon," I giggled. "It's her job to be there and see all her planning come together."

"So, I gotta pay for her to plan my wedding and pay for a plate at the wedding? Nah, Pit Pat can plan my whole shit."

"Only you would think of all of that. And she's the bride's maid, not the wedding planner." I hadn't watched the movie in a while, so I mixed up the movie with my other favorite wedding movie.I thought back to my wedding day. We had a small ceremony and it wasn't all glamorous. I was pregnant, and my feet were swollen, so I didn't enjoy myself.

Just because my marriage with Grand went to hell, I wasn't giving up that I'd marry a man that would cherish me and help me raise Gyan, like a real man was supposed to. Each time I watched this movie, it made me believe that there was a man out there that was waiting for me. A man that would cherish me and wouldn't find solace between other women's legs. Then, I was hit with reality that I was a single mother working hard to try and put a roof over both me and my kid's head.

"Let me get this straight. She's like the boss, but this other nigga over here sending her flowers and shit?"

"Yep," I snapped out of the quick slumber I had fell into. It was a hour into the movie, and I found myself dozing off. When I leaned up, I was laid up under Yoshon, and he had a fur throw laid across.

"Your ass was knocked the fuck out. How could something so beautiful snore the way you do?" He pulled my feet over the top of his legs, and I got comfortable.

Laying here cuddled in the corner didn't feel weird at all. It felt like we were just chilling and getting to know each other. My eyes were heavy and each time he asked a question, I had to pinch myself to focus on the screen. Eventually, I feel asleep and felt the covers being pulled over me as I drifted deeper and deeper into my sleep.

"Wake up, Sleepyhead," I felt Yoshon shake me gently. I woke up and the movie had ended, and he was staring at me.

"I slept through the whole movie; I was tired as hell."

"I know. I noticed you cleaned my room and shit. Just because Pit Pat is hard headed and does it, don't mean you need to. I'm a grown man and I'm capable of cleaning my own room."

Yawning, I stretched and sat up on the couch. "Your room was the least of my problems. I just came in and straightened your bed up and kept it moving."

The entire time I was speaking, he was staring right into my eyes. It caused me to blush because this look he gave me, I don't know I couldn't describe it. It was as if he was mesmerized by me or something.

"I appreciate that," he told me and touched my hand. I watched as he locked his hands into mine and bent over and kissed me on the lips. Electric sparks flew through my body when our lips met.

Breaking the kiss, I whipped the blanket off me. "No, I can't... we can't," I stammered and headed upstairs.

My head was screaming for me to get out of there and my body was yelling for me to stay right there and see where it went. I tripped up the stairs, grabbed a bottle of water from the fridge and headed to my bedroom, making sure to lock the door behind me. I couldn't.... we couldn't. This man was in a relationship, despite what he wanted to call it. Not to mention, I was staying in his home as a guest. We couldn't cross those lines and I wouldn't allow us to cross those lines. Pit Pat needed to bring her ass back here – quick. My kitten hadn't been scratched in close to a year; I didn't know how much I could avoid him. His lips... Man, his lips felt so soft and perfectly placed on mine. Then his chest, when I pushed his chest to get up, I wanted to pull him on top of me and wrap my legs around him. The thoughts that went through my head were thoughts that I couldn't afford to entertain. Going there with Yoshon only meant trouble, and the trouble would be me trying to find a place to live with my son. That was something I wasn't willing to gamble with at this moment.

13

Yoshon

THE SUN CAME CRASHING through my windows, and I was immediately pissed I forgot to put down my drapes last night. After Golden rushed out the basement like someone was chasing her, I went after her. When her door was locked, I retreated to my bedroom and fell asleep soon as I hit the bed. Eva was probably hitting my phone up like crazy and I was glad I turned my phone off. Seeing Golden in that kitchen and how she was so attentive to her son's needs made me feel a way about her. She reminded me of Ashleigh in more ways than one. The way she was domestic, yet I could tell she wasn't afraid to get her hands dirty and work. Her innocence was what made me kiss her last night. I knew it was a bold move, and I didn't know how it would end, but something inside of me wouldn't allow me to end the night without seeing what her lips felt and tasted like. Now that I had that kiss, her ass was on my mind like crazy. I kind of expected her to run away, because the shit was unexpected. When I carried her fine ass downstairs, I wasn't thinking of kissing her. Then, when I saw her stretching and how her hair was all over the place, and she had a little drool on the side of her lip, the shit made me go in for the kill.

Looking over at my alarm clock, I sighed and pulled the covers off me. It was Sunday, and although I didn't have shit to do today, I needed to power my phone on and see what the fuck had been going on while I checked out last night. Reaching for my phone, I pressed the button and watched the apple appear on the screen. Soon as it went to my home screen, a bunch of calls and text messages popped on my screen immediately. I didn't do the social media shit, so if anybody needed to get in contact with me, they had my phone number. Not too many had my number, so I knew it had to be Grape, Yolani or Eva. Scrolling through the numbers, I stopped when I heard someone at my door.

"Yo," I called out.

"It's Gyan."

"Come in," I told him and sat up on the bed with my phone in my hand. Eva's ass had left twelve messages back to back.

"Good morning. Mommy is still sleeping, so I brought you an egg sandwich." He carried a plate in the room with a cup of orange juice.

"How you know how to cook? You could have come and got me if you were hungry."

"It's okay. Mommy taught me how to make eggs when I was five. She told me I needed to learn how to cook so when I got a wife; my wife don't have to cook all the time."

I laughed and set my phone down to accept the plate. "Thank you, lil' man. I appreciate this. Did you eat?"

"Yeah, I ate before I brought you and Mommy's food up. You're welcome. Are you going to be busy today?"

"Nah, I was thinking of chilling for today. What about you?"

"I was going to ask mommy to take me to the zoo today, but it's closed. We've never been to the zoo here in New York."

"You're in New Jersey, and I can take you. Today seems like the perfect day to chill at the zoo."

"Yayyy! I'm going to tell mommy."

"How about you go shower and get dressed, and I'll go let your mommy know?" He nodded his head and stood there. "What's up?"

"You gonna taste the sandwich; I did work hard down there."

I let out a loud laugh because this kid was too much. He watched as I took a big bite and chewed it some. "Man, this is good." I tasted some eggshells, but it was the thought that counted.

"Yay. I'm going to shower and then we're off to the zoo. Thank you, Mr. Yoshon."

"Call me Yoshon."

"Mom says that I need to call adults Mr or Mrs. Pit Pat told me not to, and mommy said it was okay."

"Let's keep it between me and you." I smiled.

He smirked and headed out the room. I finished off the sandwich and washed it down with the orange juice. I quickly went to brush my teeth and wash my face, and then went down the hall to Golden's room. Gyan had left the door cracked, so I squeezed in, and she was still asleep with the sandwich next to her. I moved the plate out the way and replaced it with my body. She moaned when I rubbed her back and got more comfortable into the bed.

"Not right now, Gee," she moaned. Who the fuck was Gee? "Ugh, I said not right now. Let me sleep, I have to get Gyan up for school in a bit," she continued to talk in her sleep.

"I don't know about Gee, but I'm Yosh, and your son is up but ain't no school today." Soon as the words left my mouth, her eyes popped opened, and she stared at me.

"Why are you in my bed?" she questioned calmly.

I half suspected that she would overreact like she did last night. "We going to the zoo."

"The zoo, who said?"

"My main man, Gyan. He never been to a zoo out here, so we're going to one."

"It's snow on the ground. The zoo isn't going to be opened," she assumed. The zoo had been closed for the majority of the winter.

"The sun is out and it's melting. Today will be in the high forties, get up so we can go and enjoy our day." I got out the bed and headed to the bedroom door. She pulled the covers over her head and mumbled something. "You acting like I won't drag you out the bed."

When she heard me threaten to pick her ass up again, she ripped the blankets off her body and sat up in the bed. "You're lucky I don't feel like being picked up." She stared at me with squinty eyes and went into her bathroom.

Laughing, I went back to my room, so I could shower and get dressed for the day. Soon as I stepped foot into my bedroom, my phone was ringing. Sighing, I slid my finger across the screen and answered.

"Why was your phone going to voicemail all night?" she asked real calmly. Almost too calm for somebody who spent the whole night blowing up my phone.

"I was tired and didn't want no distractions, man. Pit Pat not here, so I was enjoying being alone and shit," I lied, and I could have told her what it was. However, did I really feel like telling the truth and then arguing with her ass today? Nah, lying seemed like the easiest way out.

"Well, you could have called me over, and we could have spent time together."

"It wouldn't have been me being alone. Plus, I just linked with you yesterday all day. I'm not feeling too good anyway."

"You sick? This weather has been crazy." She switched her tone. Eva was good with caring for someone. She would give her last to make sure you were fine, and it was something I could appreciate about her. Still, the smothering shit she been on lately was getting on my damn nerves. Calling me every five fucking minutes and then questioning me like we were together or some shit.

"I'm cool. I'm gonna chill out for the day and take some meds. Don't stress; you work today?"

"It's Sunday, Yoshon. The bank is closed," she got offended. Hell, TD bank opened on Sundays, I thought other banks would have followed their lead by now. "I'm going to the nail shop and then gonna check on my mama," she informed me.

"Ight, bet. So, we'll talk later. Let me go shower and get back in the bed," I fake yawned and she got the hint.

"Alright. We need to chat about Valentine's day," she reminded me like she had been reminding me for months already.

"Yeah. We'll do that." With that, I quickly ended the call.

Shorty wanted to act a damn fool when I took her out and now wanted to discuss Valentine's day. I never understood celebrating that damn day anyway. How the fuck were we celebrating love and shit when a massacre happened on the day? If you asked me, the shit didn't make no sense to me. I put my phone on the charger and then went to shower so we could enjoy our day. Eva's ass needed to chill and stop being all clingy. I liked her ass because she wasn't like that, but now she was becoming the very thing that I despised.

By the time I showered, shaped my face up and got dressed, Golden and Gyan was downstairs in the living room waiting. When I came down the stairs, Gyan stood up, excited that I was done.

"About time," he blurted and Golden shoved him. "Sorry, Mom," he apologized with his head down.

Golden stood up, and she was dressed in a pair of jeans, Ugg boots and a sweater. It was the simple shit she wore that made me attractive to her. She wasn't trying to stomp around a zoo in six-inch heels like Eva's extra ass would. She was dressed casual and it still looked good on her. The way the jeans clung to her body made me shift my dick in my pants.

"How you going to wake me up and take forever?"

"You trying to have me out here looking like fucked up and shit?"

"Ugh, okay, Diva," she giggled. "Did you want me to drive or..." Her voice trailed off.

"Nah, you can drive. I wanna be chauffeured around today. Right, G?"

"Right!" Gyan dapped me as we headed out. I set the security alarm and handed Golden the keys to my Tesla.

She hopped right behind the wheel as if she was comfortable or something. I watched as she worked the car like she been in this shit before. "Shorty, not too many people know how to work and drive a Tesla."

"Uh, I been in one before. My cousin's man had one," she stammered and focused on the road. She had already put the zoo's address into the GPS in the car and maneuvered the streets with ease.

"About last night," I tried to bring up and she put her hand up.

"We don't need to talk about that," she quickly blurted with nervousness. I could tell from the way she kept messing with a piece of hair that this conversation made her nervous.

"We don't need to talk about it right now. I'mma let you rock for now, but we finna talk about it later."

"Yeah, if you say so," she said, waving me off. Golden didn't know me. If I said we were going to have a conversation, we were going to have a conversation about the shit.

Golden backed into the parking lot with one hand. Shorty was experienced with driving my whip; she acted like she been whipping this shit around her entire life. Gyan was so excited to be at the zoo that he took off running toward the entrance of the zoo. Me and Golden walked side by side. I could tell she wanted to bring something up but kept fighting with herself if she was going to do it. Smirking, I already knew that kiss was on her mind. She knew she enjoyed that kiss as much as I enjoyed that shit. If it was up to me, I would have carried her ass up to my bedroom and finished what we started downstairs. Golden wasn't that type of woman and I realized that when she took off running to her bedroom.

"Pit Pat called this morning. She kept calling so I answered on the phone in my bedroom. Sorry, I was tired of hearing the phone."

"Nah, you good. The house phone in my bedroom is unplugged. When Pit Pat gets to calling and playing phone tag with her sisters, that shit ringing gets on my nerves. What she say?"

"She said that she's going to stay over your sister's house for a few more days. I told her I would pass on the message to you."

"Oh, word. She probably gonna be on Yolani's nerves.," I laughed. Pit Pat went over to Yolani's house a few times to help clean up after her and Hazel. Between Yolani never being home and Hazel running the salon, they never had a home-cooked meal. Pit Pat took it upon herself to go over to cook, clean and do anything they needed. This was what made her happy, so she did it with a smile on her face. Not to mention, she knew she would get to spend more time than she usually did with Yolani.

"That's cool. I know she over there treating Yolani like she's a baby."

"Your sister doesn't come around or something?"

"She does... just not often. Too busy handling business."

She smirked. "I can tell. From what her wife was explaining, I could tell that she works a lot. She do what you do?"

"What I used to do."

"Uh huh. Where's your mom?"

"Why you got so many questions? Where's your moms?" I shot back as I slid a hundred dollar bill to get into the zoo. The man handed me my change and we kept it pushing. "You got all these questions, answer some of mine."

"My mom didn't want me. I could of sworn I told you that."

"Nah, you told me about your grandmother raising you."

"Oh. Well, there you have it. What about you?"

"My pops killed my moms. Yolani witnessed the whole thing and she ain't been right since she saw that shit."

"And what happened to your pops? Is he in jail? Do you still have a relationship with him?" she continued to ask me all these damn questions.

"Can you have a relationship with someone in the afterlife?"

She looked down when I told her in so many words that the nigga was dead, and it was most definitely wasn't from natural causes. "I'm sorry," she apologized like it was her who pulled the trigger.

"What you sorry for? It's life and shit happens. Tell me about his father... what kind of nigga allows his seed and baby mama to struggle?"

"He's not in his life. It was one of those things that shouldn't have happened, but it did. I got my son out of it, so I came out winning." I could tell she didn't want to get too deep into the situation with Gyan's dad.

"Come on, let's go look at the tiger. Mama, you think we can pet them?" Gyan stared at his mother with pleading eyes.

"We'll see." She smiled and allowed him to pull her ahead of us. I walked behind them and watched as he showed her the different animals and told her things about them. Gyan was smart as hell, and I knew Golden had apart in that. She was intelligent herself, so his vocabulary and maturity was all because of her.

It had been an hour since we got to the zoo and Gyan seemed to be having the time of his life. He knew so many facts about the animals that even I had to fucking google to see if what he was speaking was true. The zookeepers were showing the kids how to handle the baby ducks, so me and Golden sat on the bench while they taught them all about the different animals.

"You done running? Or you got a few miles left in you?"

She messed around with her hair and smiled. "What do you mean?"

"I mean, you kissed me and then ran the fuck upstairs like I was the fucking devil or something."

"I kissed you? Okay, someone clearly has a issue with reality, and you kissed me."

"Ight, I can admit that. I kissed you and I liked the shit. Shit, I wanna do it again, if you would let me."

She giggled and rolled her eyes. "Yoshon, I'm not about to go through this with you. I'm not dating right now, and if I was, you wouldn't be who I would think about."

"Me? Why not? I'm a good ass dude." I acted like I was so hurt by what she said.

"You're in a relationship and I don't need to be dating someone who is basically taking care of me."

"I'm not in a relationship, and I'm not taking care of you. I pay your bills? Nah, you just staying in my crib until you're on your feet."

"Yeah, but you provide my meals, shelter and if I needed to borrow any money, you would be quick to hand it up to me. We can't date."

I moved closer to her and placed a kiss on her cheek. She tried to jump up but I snatched her down and pulled her on top of my lap. Placing a kiss on her lips, she allowed me and didn't put up a fight. In fact, I felt her pucker her lips up for one of the kisses I placed on her lips. When I was done, I allowed her to sit up, and she couldn't even get the words she needed to out of her mouth.

"When I want something, I get what I want. It don't matter how long or what I got to do, I'm gonna get what I want, and you got my ass wanting you."

"You don't want me, Yoshon. I'm just a woman that don't have her shit together, trying to piece it back together. You like the idea of me."

"Fuck the idea of you. I want to fuck the shit out of you, then make you breakfast in bed because that's the type of nigga I am." She was about to say something, and I stood up.

Long as she knew that I was going to be after her ass, that's all that mattered. Last night that kiss did some shit to me. I spent the night tossing and turning and debating if I should creep down the hall and wake her ass up. Instead, I went to sleep and prepped myself for the morning. As I neared Gyan and the other kids, I could tell she was still there stuck on stupid thinking about what I told her. At the end of the day, when I wanted something, I got it, and Golden was who I wanted. Yeah, I had the situation going with Eva, but all I needed was shorty to give me the word, and that would be a wrap.

14

Hazel

"WHY CAN'T we just lay down and hang out? Every time I come over here, you're trying to get me to make life-altering decisions because we fucked. It's not fair, Denim." I sat up in the bed naked as the day I was born.

He came out the bathroom from brushing his teeth. I admired his body and licked my lips. If I wasn't so upset with him, I could go another round in the sheets. Each time I came over, he wanted to talk about what I was doing with my marriage to Yolani. Right now, I didn't have all the answers he wanted me to have, and I wished I did. I wished I could tell him that I was going to get a divorce, move out our home and be alright. Those were all things I couldn't answer right now. One day I loved Yolani, and the next day, she would come home early with flowers and wanted to cuddle in the living room while watching our favorite movies. When she did things like that, it was what made me love and miss what we had. Yolani was home a lot more, and that meant my time with Denim was more limited, which didn't make him happy. I understood that while she was running the streets, he was the person who was there for me.

Denim was my escape and the reason I ran to the comfort of his arms when me and Yolani were on the outs. He was becoming a stress in my life with all his questions and shit he expected me to do. How did he think I could just finish a marriage just off the word of him? He wanted to be with me and he didn't have a problem expressing that.

"Nah, what the fuck I'm not about to be is your fuck buddy. When shit gets tough at home, you come here for some dick and to be consoled. That's not what the fuck I'm here for!" he raised his voice at me.

"You know that's not true," I ripped the blankets from my legs and stood up. "I come because you know I care for you."

"Yeah, how much? Your ass only wanna be bothered when her ass dip the fuck out to check on business. Then you on my line whispering to me about how much you miss and can't wait to see me. Hazel, you on some bullshit, for real."

"I'm on some bullshit? You're on some bullshit. You want me to drop everything I've ever known to come and be with you. In what life do people do that?"

"People in fucking love."

"How do you expect me to pick? I love my fucking wife. She's dead ass wrong with the way she moves, but I love the shit out of her and can't give up on her... on her." My chest heaved up and down because I was scared. Denim had this look in his face that told me he was fed up.

He wanted me to be flaunting my affair around like the shit was cute. When Mo told me that I needed to be careful, I should have listened to her. He cared about me and cherished me just like I wanted. Instead, I bickered and fought him over his love, and went home and tolerated Yolani's ass. What was with us women? When we had a good man standing in our face, we continued to mess around with what we knew wasn't good for us.

"Just like her ass swung you on the fucking floor and went out to do what the fuck she wanted. Who did you call? Who ran you a hot bath and made love to you all night? I did, Hazel. What you're missing is that I love the shit out of you and I've never stopped. We were supposed to be married with a kid, not you with this chick. I gotta sit back and watch the love of my life get walked on by someone who took vows to love her. The shit ain't fair, ma." I tried to grab him, and he snatched his arm away from me.

"I'm trying, Denim. You're not seeing things from my point of view. You're not seeing that I'm the one who has to make these decisions, not you. I have to leave my wife and make sure it's something that I can live with."

"Make sure it's something that you can live with?" He screwed his face up and walked out the bedroom. I grabbed a shirt and followed him into the living room.

"Yes. You don't know how much pressure I have on me right now. I have to be the one that's fine with ending a marriage. I didn't get married to get divorced, Denim. What would my parents think? Did you ever think about that?"

"Stop fronting like your parents like your wife. They might throw your ass a party," he snickered and poured him some orange juice.

"It doesn't matter if they like or dislike her ass. I'm married to her and that would fuck with their lives too. It's a lot that has to go into consideration, and you're not being fair."

My phone rang from the other room, so I went to answer it. Before I could grab it, Denim rushed into the bedroom and snatched my phone. "Tell me why I shouldn't answer this shit and tell her that you're mine."

"Because I'm not yours, Denim. I'm married!" I screamed and snatched my phone. From his expression, I could tell I hurt him.

He was in his feelings as he left back out the bedroom and I answered the phone.

"Yes, Yolani?"

"Why you gotta answer the phone like that, sexy?"

I blushed slightly. It had been a while since she showed me the attention that she was showing me lately. "I'm finishing stuff up at the shop and then heading home. Why? What's up?"

"I'm wrapping up shit on my end too. I wanna take you out to dinner tonight, so go home and get sexy," she told me.

I knew I shouldn't have been smirking in this phone like a school girl, but I was. My wife was finally doing stuff that I wanted her to do. Was I wrong to be so excited? It made me want to work on my marriage. Yolani was flawed, and I didn't want to give up on her, but I also didn't want to let Denim down too. My heart was with him too. All my old feelings I thought had gone away had come flourishing back into my heart. The way he was so patient and caring when it came to me made me fall for him even more. Whenever I was around him, I never had to lift a finger. I never had to hint about wanting to go out, because he already had plans and was just waiting for me to get off work. It was night and day when it came to Yolani and Denim. Still, I loved them both, and I felt like a boulder was sitting on my shoulder because I didn't know what to do.

"Awe, where we going, babe?" Just as I said those words, Denim walked into the bedroom and just stared at me.

"We're going to Prime 112," she disclosed.

"Um, babe, that's in Miami... how t—"

"Different state, I don't care. Get sexy because my friend is allowing me to use his jet. Don't pack clothes because we'll buy clothes when we get there," she informed me and the butterflies in my stomach was swirling.

"What about the salon and Pit Pat?"

"Pit Pat is going to stay and watch the crib, and you pay all these people to run the salon. They can handle it for a few days.

We need some time away and I'm ready to have my wife all to myself," she said all the right things to me.

"Okay, let me finish handling this, and then I'll meet you at home." I smiled. There was no hiding the smile that Yolani Santana had put on my face.

"Bet. I love you." She told me.

"Love you too, Lani," I cooed and ended the call.

I gathered my clothes and got dressed quickly. Miami was the quick trip that I needed to put everything into perspective. Holding my heels in my hand, I headed into the kitchen where Denim was sitting with scotch in a cup.

"Hey, may—"

"I'm straight, Hazel. You don't need to *handle* anything. We're good, go ahead and go home to your wife," he told me, not bothering to even look my way.

"Why are you really being like this right now? What am I supposed to tell her? No?"

"Nah, you told her what you needed to. I got shit to do, so if you're done I need to go shower and go *handle* that," He stood up and headed to the front door. The look on his face told me that he was hurt and lashing out at me. Maybe a few days away wasn't just good for me and Yolani, but also for me and Denim as well.

"I'm sorry. We'll talk in a few days, okay?" I tried to reach up and kiss his lips, but he turned his head, and it landed on his neck.

"Sayless," was all he said as I slipped my heels on and exited out the door. I hated to see that expression on his face. It especially hurt because I knew I was the one who put it there.

Soon as I got into my car, I dialed Mo's number. She answered after a few rings and sounded like she had been asleep. "You were sleep?"

"Yeah, I was up studying all night, and I got Legend down after he spent all night with a fever. What's going on, love?"

It didn't matter what she had going in her life; she would

always make time for me. Mo's house could be on fire, and she would be trying to put the fire out while helping me with my issues. It was one of the things that I loved the most about her. They didn't make people like her anymore and I was glad I had her by my side.

"Awe, give him a kiss for me. I can call back later and let you get some sleep."

"No, you're fine. I need to be waking up, so I could get these kids something to eat for dinner," she yawned. "What's going on with you? I don't like how you sound." It was another thing I loved about her. She could always tell when I wasn't myself.

"Me and Denim got into an argument about Yolani again."

I smirked because I could see her rolling her eyes up in her head. "About what this time? He knows you're married, so what is he complaining about now."

"He doesn't complain. He's just... frustrated. We'll talk in a few days when I get back from Miami."

"Um, what? The hell are you going to Miami for?"

"Well, Yolani wants us to spend a few days together there. She planned this whole romantic dinner for the both of us."

"You sound excited."

"I am excited. You know she doesn't do things like this. I feel like she's finally understanding what I'm talking about and applying it."

"Hmm. Let me guess; she called right when you were fresh off Denim's dick?"

"You don't have to make it sound like that," I snapped as I pulled onto the highway. There was traffic, but not too much where I couldn't make it home to shower and change before Yolani made it home.

"You're being stupid and not thinking right now, Hazel. I know I've told you that you need to be selfish, but you're being stupid and selfish at the same time. This man is feeling the hell out of you, and you're feeling him as well. Anytime home isn't right, you rush into his arms, and he's been there for you. You expect him to fucking sit there and be happy that you're going to spend a few days in the sun with your wife?"

I didn't expect him to be excited or even happy. However, I did expect him to deal with it. He knew I was married when he decided to fuck me into bliss that night. Even after, he knew and continued to be there for me. What was I supposed to do? End shit with my wife because the mere mention of her made him upset?

"He knew what it was before we started fucking around, Mo. Why are you putting it all on me?"

"I'm not. You're the only one who can control it, and you're not. You're playing both sides of the fence when you want to. When Yolani pisses you off, you run right to him. Then when he's applying pressure for you to choose if you want to leave Yolani, you're pissed with him. You can't have shit both ways when you're dealing with two people with feelings."

"Why do I even bother to call you?"

"Because you know that I'm right. You also know that I'm not about to sugarcoat anything. Denim is who you were supposed to be with. It doesn't mean you're supposed to be with him now. Yolani is who you married, and that doesn't mean you have to be with her either. You need to take time for yourself first."

"I hear you," I sighed.

"I hope so. Enjoy your time in Miami. The Lord knows that you need the time away from the shop. I'll hold down the fort and make sure business is conducted as usual."

"What would I do without you?"

"Who knows, just know you will never be without me."

"Love you, Mo," I smiled.

"Love you too. Call me when you land in Miami, safe flight," she told me before we ended the call.

With the rush hour traffic, it didn't take me too long to get home. When I made it home, I was happy that Yolani hadn't made it back to the house yet. Turning the key in the door, I placed my purse on the foyer table and headed straight to the stairs. When I heard the sounds of slippers sliding across the wooden floors, I knew it was Pit Pat ready to ask me where I been and if I wanted something to eat.

"Where you going, child? You forget that I'm here." She smiled, exposing the one dimple she had on her left cheek.

"I'm going to shower. Today was a busy day," I lied. Since I knew I was spending the day with Denim, I opened the shop and headed to his condo shortly after.

"Busy means money. Yolani told me about your little trip," She smiled because more than anyone, she knew how much I wanted my wife to do these things.

"Yes, I'm excited to relax and spend time with just the both of us together. It's way overdue."

"It is. I told you my hardheaded granddaughter would get it together. It may have took some time, but she is going to get it together. She loves you, Hazel."

"I know she does." I smiled and came down a few steps to hug Pit Pat. She hugged me and then had a unfamiliar look on her face.

"That scent unisex?" she asked.

"Huh?"

"Yoshon has that same cologne... it's unisex, ain't it?" Shit! She smelled Denim's cologne on me. When I walked through the door of his condo he was all over me. His cologne was all over me and I hadn't noticed.

"I sprayed some of Yolani's by accident this morning and it has been driving me nuts." I quickly covered my tracks up.

"Okay... are you hungry?"

"No, I'm going to shower and get ready to go out with Yolani tonight," I quickly headed back to the stairs. "You need to go and rest your feet. The house is spotless, and you have cooked, so you need to go and rest, Pit Pat."

"I'm tired of you children trying to tell me what to do. I'm older than all y'all butts. Leave me be." She waved me off and headed back into the kitchen, where I knew she would be.

When she rounded that corner, I ran up those stairs like a kid sneaking in after curfew. I ripped the clothes off and jumped my ass right into the shower. The water fell down my body, and I leaned my head back and allowed it to run over my hair as well. Pit Pat wasn't a fool and I wasn't sure if she believed what I said, or she was just playing dumb for the time being. I had been careful when it came to having my side relationship with Denim. He didn't have my personal cell number, and he only called my business phone. Even then, the number was never saved and I made sure to delete all our text messages. It wasn't like Yolani checked my phones anyway, but I just wanted to be careful and make sure I wasn't being sloppy.

It was no secret that people told me about the women Yolani were involved with. It never came to my front door, so I never had a reason to accuse her. How could I continue to bring her the rumors I heard in my shop? While she was doing her dirt, I was going to do mine. The only difference was that I didn't plan on stopping what I had with Denim. It felt nice to feel wanted, loved and cuddled. He made me feel like a queen and like I could rule the world with just his love alone. If I could merge both he and Yolani's good traits, I would have the perfect person. Life didn't work like that, so I had to play with the cards life dealt me.

I SAT across from Yolani as we placed our order with the waiter. It seemed like everyone was in Miami. The flight on the private jet was the highlight of my night. You only saw shit like that on the Kardashian show, and I felt real special stepping off the jet and having a Rolls Royce waiting for us. Yolani went all out to show me a good night tonight, and I couldn't wipe the smile off my face. We had a hotel suite in the Four Seasons and she had a personal shopper picking out some options for us to go on a yacht tomorrow. Whatever this woman had up her sleeve, I was so down for it. This wasn't like her so I was going to soak up all that she was giving me while we were away. Once we made it back home, I knew it was going to be back to business, and I was fine with that. A few days of R&R was what we both needed, and I planned to soak it all up until we hopped back on that jet and made it back to New York.

"I'm surprised you not hounding me about Valentine's days in two days," she brought up as she took a sip of her champagne. I was so consumed with my double life that I hadn't noticed that my favorite holiday was coming up. Maybe I did realize and I was torn on who I would spend it with. Denim wanted to do a lot but I told him to hold off on his plans until I was sure what I was going to do.

"We'll back in the city by then," I smiled. "I've had a lot on my plate with the shop, so I don't even know what day it is half the time." That statement did hold some truth to it, yet it wasn't about my shop, it was more about which person I was going to choose to lay up with. When Yolani didn't come home, I would leave and head to Denim's crib. With Pit Pat staying with us for a few, I couldn't ease out as much as I wanted without her being so damn nosey.

Yolani reached across the table and grabbed my hand. She gently rubbed them while staring into my eyes. "I fucked up. A lot of shit I fucked up on and I promise I'm gonna make it better."

"This is a step in the right direction, babe. Neither of us have been perfect in our marriage. I just want us to get to a place where we can speak about it without neither of us running out and not wanting to discuss stuff. We can't keep sweeping stuff under the carpet and ignoring it. Especially you; you shut me out so much, Yolani."

"Yeah, I hear you. Shit don't be easy to sit and talk about shit with you. You don't understand that I need to be in the streets. It's where my money is tied and how we survive, feel me?"

"What you have to understand is that I get all of that. I know that's how we survive, but you don't need to be out there for everything. You have a team and you need to trust that they will handle what needs to be handled while you're away. My team at the salon makes sure everything is handled, even before I hear about the stuff. While you're trying to be everything to the streets, you're lacking in your home."

"I'm gonna try and do better," she promised me. I needed her to do more than promise me. She needed to actually apply the shit I was saying to her. This wasn't going to work unless we both tried, and I couldn't go off her, and the word try.

"I need more than you trying. Yolani, you need to actually do this. Babe, I'm this close to calling it quits, I swear." Tears streamed down my eyes. Staring into her eyes the love I had for her was there and would never leave. Why was it so easy to tell her that I wanted to leave, but actually leaving was something I couldn't do?

"Why you crying, Ma?" She stood and leaned across the table to wipe my tears. I had no intentions on crying. I guess it happened when you were so tired of holding everything in, and your wife tells you she would *try* to be better in y'alls marriage.

"You don't know how hard it is to wake up and try to keep a smile on your face. It's hard as fuck because I have to head to work and act like my entire life isn't falling apart, Lani. You head out, and you're gone all day, and you don't think to check in with me, or even come home from dinner."

"Babe, I'm home for dinner and all night now," she tried to counter like her recent behavior change changed everything that she did in the past.

"You just recently started doing that. What about before? You would be gone for days and then show up to shower, and you're back in the streets. I feel like we're not on the best terms and it hurts."

"I can't speak on my actions in the past. I'm going to be better when it comes to you and our marriage. I'm not perfect, and I'm gonna fuck up and shit, but you got my word that I'm gonna give this shit my all."

"Promise?"

"I promise, Stinky," she called me by my nickname that only she was allowed to call me. Standing up, she reached across the table and placed a kiss on my lips.

I'm done with this shit. You want to work on your marriage, then I'm falling back and allowing you to do that shit. Don't call or text this number because I'm changing this number tomorrow. Just when shit was getting sweet with me and Yolani, here comes Denim with his bullshit. I didn't understand how these men juggled more than one woman. Here I was struggling with a man and woman, and I felt like I was going to pull my hair out and scream.

Stop being like this. I'll see you and we'll talk when I get back. I waited for him to reply and he never did. Slipping the phone back into my purse, I turned my attention back to Yolani who was staring at me.

"What happened?"

"What you mean?"

"Your whole facial expression changed and shit. You good?"

"Yeah. One of my clients is pissed I'm out of town. I forgot I booked her whole entire wedding party. I left her in good hands anyway; she'll be fine."

"You sure? We can fly back so you can handle your business and come back."

"Babe, how am I going to handle business when I'm complaining to you about business? I'm fine, and we're enjoying ourselves, no business."

"No business." She sniffled and rubbed her nose.

"Are you getting sick? You've been sniffling since we got on the jet in New York," I pointed out.

"Yeah, I think I'm fucking coming down with something." She rubbed her nose and then finished the rest of her champagne.

"You need to order some soup when we get to the hotel. Knock it out before it gets worse. Should have told Pit Pat, she would have had something ready for you."

She laughed. "Nah, that shit would have me sweating out my ass. I'm good on her old remedies. I'll get some medicine at the hotel and chill tonight. I'll be good for tomorrow."

"Okay" I smiled.

While on this date and enjoying Yolani's company, I couldn't help but to stare down at my phone to see if Denim had messaged me back. He hadn't, and although I should have felt like I was on top of the world, I didn't. I wanted him to message me back. I wanted to know everything between us was alright and that we could fix it when I got home. Only time would tell if I would be able to fix what I did. Knowing Denim, I would be able to fix our situation soon as my feet hit the pavement in New York City.

15

Yolani

"RIGHT THERE, BABY," Hazel moaned as I licked her in all the right places. I had her legs up to the headboard as I had my tongue damn near in her ovaries. She kept trying to run from the tongue, but I held her ass right in place. She wasn't escaping shit when it came to me. It had been a while since I was able to stick my tongue up in my honey pot, and vacation was the perfect time to get a little taste. "I'm about to cum, Babe! I'm 'bout to..." her voice trailed off as her legs went limp.

"Told you to stop playing with me." She rolled her eyes as I winked and then kissed her second set of lips. Hazel liked to play games like tasting her wasn't my favorite shit to do.

"You get on my nerves," she giggled and closed her legs while pulling the covers over her. "Where you going?" she questioned when she noticed me putting on my robe.

"I'm gonna go smoke a cigarette real quick."

"Cigarette? I thought you quit months ago, Yolani." She leaned up, alarmed that I had mentioned a cigarette.

"I did. Shit just been stressing me and I picked it back up. I'm gonna quit again for good; I got you."

"Hurry up so I can rub my cold feet on you." She tossed a pillow at me as I left the bedroom. Sliding the balcony door open, I took a seat on the balcony and looked around quickly. Pulling the baggy out, I shook some out on the side of my hand and took a deep sniff. Leaning back, I held my nose and coughed a bit.

If Hazel knew I was out on the balcony doing coke instead of smoking a cigarette, she would have lost her shit. I told myself I was going to quit the coke. Each time I tried some shit always happened, and it caused me to take a sniff just so I could function. With Cherry in the hospital, that shit had me stressing more than usual. When I went up there to see her, her eyes got big as saucers, and she tried to claw all her shit out of her body. With a tube down her throat, she couldn't speak on why she was trying to rip out everything out of her arm. After I told her what would happen to her sister, she calmed herself down and understood that she better keep my mouth out of this shit. The cops were up there every day to question her and ask if she could remember anything. I knew if my name came up, I would do worst to her and she wouldn't get the chance to breathe another whiff of air on this precious earth.

The reason I decided to come to Miami was to get away for a while. I needed a break from New York and a few days to just sit back and truly enjoy life. With all the work I put in, you would think I would spend my money on lavish trips and vacations. The only thing lavish I saw was the inside of my house. Other than that, I saw the hoods of Brownsville, Brooklyn. See, I was about to dip and then call Hazel when I landed. When I thought of getting away, I thought of being alone and able to do coke when I wanted to and party with some bad bitches here in Miami. It was the reason my ass paid 30k to fucking use my friend's private jet.

Flying commercial wouldn't have allowed me to bring my shit with me. Me and Hazel been on good terms and she wasn't stressing me out. Her ass was a little too quiet and it had me worried. Nah, my baby wouldn't cheat or do no shit like that.

When I realized that Valentine's day was near, I knew I had to bring her along and do things that she deserved. We were at a point where we didn't say shit to each other. Hazel was my heart, and I know I didn't always do good by her, I did love the shit out of her. Everything that I did I thought about her and how it would fuck with our household. It was the reason we had that house and she drove a foreign car. Not to mention, she never had to worry about shit from her salon because I covered it all. Everything she made, she pocketed that shit and put into her accounts. We had separate accounts because I wasn't ready to make that leap and add both our names to my account. Hazel would never snake me. Still, I had trust issues that I wasn't ready to deal with now. As of right now, she thought I didn't have enough time to head to the bank and open a joint account.

I took another sniff and then headed back into the room. When I came into the room, Hazel was knocked out cold. She talked all that shit about wanting to watch a movie and cuddle, and her ass was in here sucking up all the good air with her snores. I shook my head and climbed into bed beside her. I watched as she nuzzled close to me and then kissed me on the neck.

"I love you, baby," she told me and placed her arms around me. She loved the shit out of me and I knew it. Any other bitch would have been gone with only half the shit I put her through. Still, she stuck around and tried to fix and understand me when she didn't have to. It was something she didn't have to do and here she was trying to fix something I kept shitting on in her face.

"Ma, I love you so much." I kissed her forehead and pulled the cover closer onto us. We needed to have a night like this every night. My high was kicking in and I felt like I was on top of the world right now. My ass wasn't even tired, I was just high and staring at the damn ceiling. This shit had me feeling all numb and shit. It almost felt like the first time I took a sniff in the back of my whip with one of my workers. When that nigga tried to out me, I popped his head off, and now he was six feet under. Yoshon had to go to his damn funeral and didn't even know why the fuck he was going. This little nigga had loose lips and that's why I permanently made sure they would be shut. I could stop doing this shit whenever the fuck I wanted, I wasn't addicted. The shit took the edge off and allowed me to calm down every once in a while. On the real, it calmed my anxiety too.

Hazel ripped the blankets off me and jumped on the bed. By the time my high wore off, the sun was peeking over the water. My damn head felt like it was about to explode if she didn't close those blinds and let me get some more sleep.

"Babe, you went to sleep with me last night, how are you still tired?"

"I couldn't sleep so I went and sat on the balcony until a little after four. What time is it?" I pulled the covers over my head and sighed in relief.

"It's ten in the morning. The personal shopper is coming in a few minutes with the clothes she pulled for us. You need to get up so we can try everything on."

"Babe, I'm not gonna hold you, I'm tired as fuck and feel like I'm gonna be sick if I don't go back to sleep. We got the yacht later and I don't want to be in a bad mood." If she didn't get the fuck out this room, our entire trip was about to be fucked up, because I was ten seconds from cursing her the fuck out.

"Fine, I'll try on my clothes and then go grab some breakfast. Mo's cousin lives out here so we'll do breakfast and some more shopping."

"Yeah, whatever, have fun," I mumbled under the blankets and waved her ass out the bedroom. She closed the door behind her and I squeezed my eyes shut to finish getting some sleep before later on today. The way I was feeling, I needed to fucking sleep, or anybody around me was liable to get cursed the fuck out.

BETWEEN HAZEL CONTINUING to burst in the bedroom to use the mirror while trying on clothes, and then her and Mo's loud ass cousin laughing and catching up, I was irritated. Fuck the boat, fuck Miami and fuck life, that was how I was feeling. Even though I was feeling like that, I had to suck it up and show Hazel a good time. I promised that I would work on myself and I wanted to keep my promise. Let it had been a few days ago, and she would have been crying on a plane back home because I wouldn't have hesitated on letting her know how I feel. Quietly, I put my sneakers on and stared at myself sitting on the bed through the mirror. Not too bad for a chick that was born and raised in the hood. I wore a white Versace button down, plaid shorts and a fresh pair of all white Yeezy boost.

"You clean up very well." Hazel came out the bathroom putting her earring into her ear. She wore a pink sundress that clung to every curve she had on that fine ass body of hers. On her feet, she wore a pair of gold sandals that came up her thighs. The slit on the side of her dress showed the detail of her sandals. She had just got out the shower, so she had her hair curly, wet and wild. Shorty looked good as fuck, and I was ready to rip this dress off and stay our ass in the crib tonight.

"Talking about me and you over here about to get banned from stepping out in that tonight." I licked my lips as I stared at my wife looking all good and shit. Her booty bounced with each step she took. I was ten minutes from telling her ass that we weren't going nowhere with her in that damn dress.

"I look good, don't I?" she spun around and propped her hand on her thick hip. "Well, Pit Pat called me a bunch of times since earlier. When I called her back, she told me she would speak to me when we got home."

"You know Pit, she's dramatic and probably found a ant in the crib and want to call an exterminator," I waved it off.

Being raised by my grandmother, I already knew about her dramatics. She had OCD and cleaned any and every damn thing. Once I was old enough and could afford to move out, I was out. Yoshon had always been her favorite, and that's why he chose to have her move in with him instead of buying her a home. She babied the shit out of us and I hated that shit. Yeah, it was nice to have her do shit that I didn't feel like doing, but she always questioned me on shit I knew to do. Don't get me wrong, I loved the shit out of my grandmother and would lay down and die for her. It was something about immigrant grandparents that screamed overbearing. When she came over a couple times a week it was good enough with me. She usually would bother Hazel with anything and everything since I stayed gone.

"Yeah, I guess," she touched her neck with a worried expression on her face. "Yeah, you're right, she is dramatic." She tried to convince herself.

"You alright?"

"Uh huh. I'm fine," she said and spritzed some perfume onto her wrist. "You ready to go? What exactly will we be doing on this yacht?"

"Chill, you don't need to worry about that right now," I told her as I grabbed her hand and led her out the hotel room.

We made our way downstairs and caught a town car to the docks to board the yacht. I walked around the whip and opened the door for Hazel. She looked beautiful as she stared up at me as I helped her out the car. My phone buzzed, and I looked at the caller ID and it was Cherry's sister. Ignoring the call, I helped Hazel onto the boat as the captain and the catering team greeted us.

"Thank you for choosing us to show you around Miami, Mrs.

And Mrs. Santana," he greeted us. He had white hair and a beard, and his skin had seen better days. It looked as if he sat under the sun all day and didn't bother to use sunscreen.

"Thank you for having us." Hazel smiled and shook his hand.

"If you follow me, we have you set up right in front of the sun, so that you can see how beautiful the sunset is. We also have a delicious meal that's being prepped and ready for you," he explained as he held out the chair for Hazel.

"I got it." I stopped him from holding out the chair for me. Sitting my phone facing down on the table, I looked out at the water. The waiter poured champagne in both our flutes and Hazel smiled.

"Thank you."

"This shit is dope. Worth all the money I paid to have this shit to ourselves." They had a nice little setup and it was nice to be on the water, sipping champagne and enjoying each other's company.

All of this should have been enough for me, but it wasn't. I had a itch that I needed to scratch, and I needed to find the nearest bathroom. "It is. You okay, babe? Your nose is bleeding," she pointed out. I thought my shit was just running, but it was actual blood pouring from my nose.

"Shit, let me go to the bathroom and clean this shit up," I jumped up and Hazel tried to come with me. "Babe, sit and enjoy yourself. I'm good."

I rushed off into the bathroom and held my nose with some tissue. It was bleeding for a good ten minutes before it stopped completely. I paced the bathroom with the baggie of coke wondering if I should snort just a little. I had never experienced nose bleeds and I didn't want this shit to start back up. I placed the baggie in my pocket with the other two I had stored there and headed back out to where Hazel was sitting. When I got to the table, she was no longer sitting there, instead she was standing with a glass of champagne while staring out at the water. We hadn't took sail yet, so the boat was rocking slowly on the waves while still being docked.

"Beautiful, ain't it?"

She took a sip of her champagne and nodded her head. "You left your phone on the table over there." My heart fell in the pits of my shoes. How the fuck did I slip up like that? My fucking bloody nose made me forget about my phone that I sat on the table.

"Got a real interesting call while you were in the bathroom," she continued and guzzled the rest of her champagne. "Who the fuck is Cherry and why does her sister feel the need to inform you on how she's doing in the hospital?"

I could either lie or I could tell her the truth. Only a fucking dummy would sit there and tell the truth. Obviously, Cherry's sister didn't into detail, so I was still in the clear to swing this shit how I wanted.

"Ma, you tripping over Cherry? For what? Her sister better tell me what's going on with her because she was beat the fuck up and robbed while making deliveries for me. I want to know if this shit was planned or she was really attacked."

Her face calmed down and she held onto her glass. "Why didn't you tell me about that? I thought this was some side bitch or something."

If she only knew the laugh I was doing was a fucking nervous laugh, she would have backhanded the shit out of me. "Nah, Cherry is good people. Shit, I hope because I'd hate to send her to God anytime soon."

She sat the cup down on the railing and came over to hug me. "I'm sorry. You know I get crazy when it comes to you."

Kissing her on the lips, I sighed in relief because I had pulled myself out some deep shit. God had my back with how I was able to finesse my way out of this situation. Hazel was pleased and that's all that mattered. This trip needed to be a good one, and I wasn't trying to fuck anything up.

16

Golden

I SAT behind Yoshon's desk and went over the employment applications for his tanning salon. It felt nice to finally have something to do other than sitting around the house and wiping the kitchen counters down every five minutes. He handed me a stack of applications and told me to go through them and call who I felt fit the job descriptions in for an interview. While I worked, he sat on the couch in his office watching highlights from the basketball last night with his laptop and phone beside him. Although he was supposed to be chilling, he still was working and answering calls.

After my third sigh, he turned around and stared at me before he spoke. "You good? Need me to come over there and give you a massage?"

"I think I can manage, Yoshon. You're my boss; you want me to file a sexual harassment suit?"

"Nah, I'm just trying to make sure my employee is cool and comfortable," he chuckled. "On the real, I'm hungry as fuck."

"I have some salmon patties I made for breakfast left. I can put them over a salad for lunch," I offered.

From him licking his lips and rubbing his hands, I already knew his answer so I placed the application I was going over down. "Yeah, shit sound good as fuck."

"It does now that I'm sitting here thinking on it. I'll bring it in here and we'll have a working lunch."

"Bet." He turned his attention back to the TV and I went to make lunch.

From his kiss the other night and the kiss at the zoo, things weren't weird between us. I guess because he already stated that he wanted me, and I knew that he did. All I was interested in was making some money, so I could afford some place for me and my son. I appreciated Yoshon for all he did, but long as I was living under his roof, I couldn't be involved with him. Each time he spoke, I watched his lips and wanted to suck on his lips while I rode his dick. When I went past his bedroom, I wanted to turn the knob and drop my clothes and show him how nasty I could get. The thoughts that ran through my head about this man shouldn't have been thoughts running through my head. Our kiss... it was something that I thought about all the time. Why was I so consumed with one stupid kiss from this man?

He was my knight in shining armor. He saved me from something I wasn't sure I'd be able to do alone. I was strong and could handle as much that comes at me. That night when he found me, I was weak. I didn't know how I was going to survive for myself and my son. How was I going to keep us warm in this car for the winter? When my car broke down, I didn't know what I would do. As a mother, we were supposed to find solutions for our babies. They looked at us for answers and we had to pull a solution out of thin air. At that moment, if my son asked me what we were going to do, I had no answer for him. Yoshon came along and pulled me out the hole that seemed to continue to get deeper and hasn't asked for anything. My son loved him and would spend hours talking history, animals and anything else. Yoshon was different from street dudes and it's what I liked about him.

He had the swagger and hood about him, but then he could sit down and talk about history and other stuff. With him being older, I could tell he didn't have time for the games and knew what he wanted. When he left the house, he wasn't gone for days and didn't come in with no explanation. He went out to handle his business and made it home for dinner every night. We've fell into these roles while Pit Pat was gone. If he was going to be late for dinner, he would call me and tell us to eat without him. If he was really late, I would leave his food in the microwave with a note. It was a routine that we fell into and neither of us spoke on it. It just worked for us, so there was no need to speak on it.

"I left the salmon cake cold so that it would go with the salad better," I handed him a plate and leaned up. Walking over to his desk, I sat my food down and got right to business with these applications. With all Yoshon had done for me, I didn't want to let him down with this job. Anything he needed, I wanted to make sure I was on my job.

"Damn, these shits were good as fuck this morning and they're better now." He chewed loudly while smacking on his food.

"The door. I'll get it," I stood up. "It's probably a package that needs to be signed for," I told him and went to the door.

My slippers slid across the wooden floors as I made my way to the front door. Looking through the glass was a woman with a short pixie cut, standing there with bowls in her hand. Opening the door, I smiled at her and wondered who the hell she was.

"Hey, can I help you?" I politely questioned her.

"Um, who are you? Is Yoshon here?" she asked as she tried to stare around me into the house.

"He's here. Can I ask who you are?"

"Eva, his girlfriend," she felt the need to toss in there. This man hadn't lie to me yet, and couldn't stand lying, so I knew she was adding more into their relationship than he was. Yoshon had told me a million times that he didn't have a girlfriend and he was just messing with someone.

"Ohhh, yes, his *friend*, Eva. Follow me, we were just having lunch while working," I spoke as we walked through the house. "Do you want some water?" We stopped in the hall and I fixed a sculpture on the table.

This woman looked so offended as if I was asking her if her hair was real. I could tell that me acting like I was familiar with this house was pissing her off. Meanwhile, all I was trying to do was help her out with some water or something. We walked into Yoshon's office, and he looked over his shoulder and saw me with Eva. Any other man would have spit his drink out, sat up or jumped up, but he was cool as a cucumber.

"What's good, Eva? What you doing here?"

"I made you some homemade soup and tea. Thought I'd drop it off and spend the day with you because I'm off today."

"Oh word? You should have called before coming over," he told her as I sat back at the desk. Tossing another application in the trash, I continued to go through the pile. All I had was three solid candidates, and I needed to hire ten.

"I need to call to come visit my boyfriend?" she scoffed. I took a bite of my food and shook my head. If he was really your man, he wouldn't have questioned why the hell you showed up at his home, uninvited. Instead, it was more about trying to take an imaginary dig at me when I didn't care about her and Yoshon's situation.

"We're not together, Eva, so why you fronting?"

Her head snapped over to me and I wasn't paying attention. I was trying to figure out what the hell this person filled out. "Can you give us some privacy, please?"

Looking up, I stared at Yoshon and smiled. "Sure. I need to

concentrate anyway. I'll be in my room going over these, if you need me."

"She lives here? You failed to let me know that, Yoshon."

"Since when the fuck do I have to run who lives with me by you? You don't pay the property taxes on this bitch. Why is she even a topic of conversation?" he questioned her.

"Yoshon, you should have told me you have a woman living with you. Why do you think that this alright?"

"Eva, she's my fucking friend and assistant. Why the fuck are you tripping!" he barked. This man never raised his voice, and here he was irritated by this bitch's constant questions about me.

"I'll be upstairs. If you need me, send me a text message."

"What would he need you for?" she replied, instead of the person I was talking to. Ignoring her, I walked out the room and went upstairs. "Were you checking out her ass?" I heard her squeal and chuckled to myself.

Yoshon liked to say he wasn't in a relationship, but it was clear his ass was. Eva thought that was her man and was obviously very protective of him. What good would it do for me to become offended and want to pick a fight with her because she bothered by me? Obviously, I was already winning if my presence bothered her and I hadn't done anything to her. When I got to the bedroom, I closed the door and put the stack of papers on the nightstand and plopped on the bed. I grabbed the remote and scrolled through the channels until I found Animal Planet. It was something about animals that I loved. It was probably why Gyan loved them too. When we were settled in our own home, I wanted to get a mini pig and name him Bacon. Both me and Gyan came up with the name two years ago. Grand told me that he wasn't about to let no pig in this crib unless it was fried up in a skillet and placed on his plate for breakfast. My eyes were getting heavy as I watched a bird get prepped for surgery. Turning the volume down, I turned over on my side and decided to catch a nap before I had to go pick Gyan up from school.

I was driving his BMW now, and I went to the city to drop and pick up Gyan every morning. My car was still in the shop, and I didn't question Yoshon on when it was going to be done because I didn't have the money for a new transmission. His BMW got me around perfectly, and I was able to run errands when he needed to me grab things, or when I needed to grab things for dinner. Gyan loved the car because it was an upgrade from the Nissan we were sleeping in. I don't know how many times I had to remind him that it wasn't our car and he didn't need to be getting comfortable in it. Seeing the smile on my son's face every morning made all of this worth it. When you were independent, accepting help from someone was like pulling your lip over your face. As his mother, I wanted to pick up the slack and handle things that needed to be handled, but I had to toss in the towel and realize that I was doing more harm to my son than help. He was sleeping in a car, brushing his teeth in a gas station bathroom and grabbing free breakfast in the morning before school. Free breakfast aside, those were things he shouldn't have to deal with as a child. Yawning, I fluffed my pillows and then laid back and fell fast asleep. I'd get to the applications tonight before I went to bed.

I JUMPED up out my sleep quick with my heart racing. Staring at the clock on the nightstand, I jumped out the bed and gathered anything to go pick my son up. It was after five and I was hours late to pick up my son.

"Oh God, Oh God. I'm sorry, Gyan," I spoke to myself as I zoomed down the stairs and headed to the door.

"Where you going?" I heard Yoshon's voice from behind me.

Turning around in pure panic, I screamed. "I overslept! Why didn't you wake me up?" I screamed and turned back around.

"Calm down. I went and picked Gyan up from school. The teacher remembered me when you picked him up the other day and released him to me only if I allowed her to put my ID in his school's file."

This entire time I hadn't realized that I was holding my breath. Walking into the kitchen, I pulled my son into my arms as he ate his afterschool snack. "I'm so sorry, baby," I apologized to him over and over again.

"Mom, you were tired. You worry too much and hardly sleep."

"You're too smart for your own good. How was school today?" Yoshon leaned on the doorway and I mouthed thank you to him. It's like this man refused to let me down. I guess he was trying to prove to me that he could be there for me and wouldn't let me down.

"I know. School was fun. We're going to Washington to learn about the government and stuff. I told my teacher that I couldn't go."

"Why not?"

"It's two-hundred dollars. Mom, I know you don't have the money for the trip. It's okay; I don't want to see Trump anyway."

"Baby, you need to stop telling me what I can or cannot do. Let me be the one to decide that, you hear me?" he stared into my eyes as I held onto his cheeks. "Now, where's the permission slip? I can pull the emergency money I have in the car."

"That's just in ca—"

"I don't want to hear about it."

"It's paid for."

"What?" both me and Gyan said in unison.

"While she had me in the office filling out papers and copying my ID card, she mentioned the trip, and how she was sad Gyan said he couldn't go. I filled out the permission slip and paid for the trip. All you gotta do tomorrow is go and put your signature on the permission slip."

Gyan jumped down from the stool and ran right into Yoshon's arms. "Thank you so much, Mr. Yoshon!" His face was priceless.

My baby was so happy to be going on the trip with all his friends from school.

"Thank you, Yoshon. You didn't hav—"

"Stop telling me what I didn't have to do," he told me. "I did it because he's a good kid, and he's smart. I may not agree with the government or our president at the moment, but as a boy that's going to become a black man, he should learn all he needs to about our corrupt ass system."

"You're right. Thank you for doing this for him," I joined in on the hug.

"Damn, what else I need to buy to keep getting hugs from y'all?"

"I did want thi—"

"Gyan!" I screamed out.

After dinner, I tucked Gyan into bed. He was so excited and happy that he was going to be going on his school's trip. The boy couldn't stop talking about everything that he planned to learn about. He even convinced me to take him to the bookstore to get some books on Washington. As I pulled the covers over him, he stared at me with a smile on his face.

"Why you smiling so hard?"

"Mr. Yoshon told me that he likes you, Mom." He smirked and laughed to himself. A smile came across my face.

"Oh, did he? Mr. Yoshon is crazy."

"He's not crazy, Mom. You don't like him back?" How was I supposed to explain how complicated our situation was? It was more than me just liking him or him just liking me.

"It's more complicated than that, babe. Mr. Yoshon is an amazing man, and I appreciate all he has done for me and you."

"Me too. I wish he was more like my daddy," he whispered when he spoke about Grand. Gyan didn't really speak about his dad, and he also knew not to bring him up.

"I do too, babe. Now, get some sleep so you can ace your spelling test tomorrow. I love you, Gyan."

"Love you too, mama." I smiled and closed the door to his room and headed down to Yoshon's office. He was out back smoking a blunt and drinking his liquor. Living with him, I noticed that it was his alone time that he enjoyed, so I made sure not to bother him when he was having alone time.

"Okay, it's me and you, papers," I giggled to myself and started going through them again. It took too long for me to go through these papers. As I was picking another candidate, the house phone started to ring. Picking it up, I answered. "Hello."

"Hey Golden, baby. How is everything?" It was Pit pat checking in on her home and grandson. I had gotten used to her calls since she been over at his sister's house.

"I'm doing good... how are you doing?"

"Over here taking care of my granddaughter's house while she's in Miami with her wife... you remember her, right? Hazel."

"Yes, I remember Hazel. That's nice that they're getting some alone time together."

"Uh huh. How's my grandson doing?"

"Pit, no disrespect, but you do know he's a grown man and capable of taking care of himself? I barely do anything for him, and he's been getting along fine while you're gone." I prayed that I didn't overstep my boundaries with her.

She sighed into the phone. "I worry about him sometimes. It wasn't too long ago that he lost his fiancée, Ashleigh. She died and ever since, he hasn't been himself. I keep an eye on him to make sure he's fine."

Yoshon never mentioned anything about his fiancée to me. Maybe it was too painful and he didn't feel the need to bring her up to me. "I understand. I'm sorry if I came off rude."

"You're perfectly fine, baby. I know that you'll look out for him while I'm over here. Will you do that for me?"

"Yes, Ma'am."

"Okay, make sure to tell him that I called and will talk to him in the morning. Y'all have a good night."

"You do the same." I smiled and ended the call.

Pit Pat was a typical grandmother who worried about her grandbabies. It didn't matter how old and grown they were, she was still worried about them, and would always be. She reminded me of my grandmother a lot. She worried about me when I got with Grand, and I fought her because of it. All she wanted was the best for me and I was so worried about chasing after a man. I was so wrapped into a man that wasn't good for me that I ended my relationship with the woman who meant the world to me. The woman who raised me when my own mother wouldn't. I didn't even get a chance to say goodbye to her because I was so busy trying to be everything to someone who didn't appreciate anything. That shit ate me up every single day. There was no redo button or anything that I could press that would bring her back. It was something I had to live with for the rest of my life.

"You alright?" Yoshon's voice startled me.

Wiping the tear that slid down my cheek, I shook my head. "Yes, I'm fine. Your grandmother called and she reminds me a lot of my grandmother."

"We can go and visit her if you want," he told me.

"We can'..." my voice trailed off because I had forgotten that I told him she was in a nursing home. "I didn't want to tell you, but she's dead."

"Damn, she just died?"

"No, I lied. She been dead," I confessed.

His face was stone as he sat in the seats in front of his desk. "Why?"

"Because I'm too embarrassed to say that I went chasing after a man and ended my relationship with my grandmother because she didn't approve. She was dying and I didn't know because I was too selfish and stuck in my own ways to reach out to her." My tears slipped down my cheeks. "When I got back to New York, I wanted to work on our relationship. I wanted... no, I needed my grandmother, and I find out that she died."

He ran his hand over his face as he stood up and came around the desk. He pulled my arms and forced me to stand up. Pulling me into his arms, he allowed me to cry into his chest. "We're not perfect people. Yeah, we're going to make fucked up and stupid decisions, but it doesn't make us a bad person."

"My grandmother needed me, and I wasn't there, Yoshon. You would move hell and high water for your grandmother, and I just allowed mine to die."

"Yes, I would. Me and my grandmother aren't you and yours. Go visit her grave. You can tell she forgives you for what you did."

"How?" I stared up into his face.

"She brought me into your life. That night I found you, I wasn't even going to show up because of the snow, but something told me I needed to go."

Leaning my head on his chest, I sniffled. "Why didn't you tell me about your fiancée?" His body became tense.

"I don't like to speak about her."

"I understand."

"She died from cancer. Felt like God either didn't want me happy, or he was paying me back for all the havoc I wrecked in the streets for years. I'm not innocent and I've done some shit that I have to answer for when judgment day comes."

"Same," I replied.

We didn't say anything, we just stood there, and I was comfortable as hell. He had his arms wrapped around me, and for the first time, I felt safe in his arms. It was something about Yoshon's aura and personality that made you want to be with and around him.

"I'm sorry about Eva earlier... I told her that we needed some space apart and shit."

"You don't have to apologize to me."

"Yes, I do. She came at you sideways a few times and I need to apologize."

Looking up into his arms, I nodded my head. "It's okay."

Yoshon stared down into my eyes and then bent down and kissed me. I placed my arms around his neck and kissed him back. He put his hands on my legs and tapped them, and I wrapped them around him. Yoshon walked out the office and headed to the stairs while we continued to kiss. I wanted him right now. No more dreaming and daydreaming, I wanted the real thing, and he did too. While he climbed up the stairs, I sucked on his neck and kissed his face. When we got to his bedroom, he placed me down on the bed, softly pulling until my leggings were on the floor. I laid across his bed in my thong and T-shirt, and he stood back and admired me. Leaning over me on the bed, he kissed my lips aggressively and lifted me up out of my shirt.

"I want you bad, Golden," he growled into my ears.

"Then have me," I moaned as he played with my clit with his thumb. He stared at me as he continued to massage down there. Leaning up, I stole a kiss on his lips. "Put it in me, Yoshon," I told him.

I hadn't had sex since the day Grand raped me in our bedroom. Sex wasn't on my mind and I didn't think I would ever have the urge to want to have sex again. Yoshon Santana came walking into my life and made all my lady parts work all over again, and for that, I was grateful. When he pulled his shorts off, his dick was poking out the hole in the front of his boxers. This man was working with something my ass probably had no business trying to handle. He parted my legs and positioned himself in between my legs and kissed me. I watched as he leaned up and grabbed a condom before he pushed himself inside of my lady cave. My back arched on its own and my mouth was wide open. It felt as if I was a virgin all over again.

"Shit, I should have known something as beautiful as you would have the best pussy I've ever had." He kissed me on the neck as he inched each piece of himself inside of me. Holding onto his arms, I relaxed myself and allowed him to continue.

"Hmm, like that." I directed, and he gyrated his hips and hit all the parts that caused me to scream out in pure pleasure.

"Guess what it is?" he whispered in my ear before kissing it.

"What?" I moaned out in pure heaven. This kitten hadn't been scratched in some time, and I felt like I was on cloud nine right about now.

"It's Valentine's day." He gave me a wet and sloppy kiss right on the lips. As he sucked on my lips and delivered those deep strokes, I stared over his shoulder and looked at the clock on the dresser. Sure enough, it was after twelve and considered Valentine's day. Yoshon had no clue what he was doing to me, and then again, I had no clue what I had done to him.

17

Hazel

Miami was everything I could have dreamed of and more. Yolani and I reconnected more than I thought we would. We talked, cuddled and enjoyed each other's company. It had been a long time since we've laughed and joked with each other. It made me miss our friendship before we were married. I had forgot Yolani was so funny and sarcastic that it brought me to tears. We made love almost every day while being in Miami. On Valentine's day, she rented out an entire restaurant for me and told fourteen reasons why she loves me. It was the most romantic thing she had ever done for me. My emotions and feelings were all over the place as we left Miami. Although I was happy and feeling so special that my wife went out of her way, a part of me couldn't help to check my phone to see if Denim had responded to my messages I've sent him. He ignored me the entire trip and didn't take my calls.

Instead of ringing, his phone went straight to voicemail. I've left voicemails and apologized, and I hadn't heard anything from him. We've been back from Miami for a week, and I couldn't stop thinking about him. Yolani was back running the streets, but she made sure she came home or checked in if she wasn't going to make it home. With Denim being gone, I was trying to focus on work and convince myself not to go over to his sneaker store or condo. The exam room door opened and the doctor came into the room.

"Good morning, Mrs. Santana. How are you doing today?" He sat his file down and proceeded to wash his hands.

"I'm good, Doc. I just really need to get some form of birth control." I didn't want to continue to have sex with Denim without having some form of birth control. It was something I've been meaning to do and failed to get around to it.

"You're married to a woman, Hazel." He stared at me, confused.

"We're g—"

"Not my business," he cut me short. "I'm sorry, we can go ahead and get that done today. Take this and go pee in it. I know you're not, but we need to make sure," he told me and handed me the cup.

I went into the bathroom and quickly relieved my bladder and came back out. "Thank you. Let me go ahead and get my nurse to administer the test. Other than this, how is everything?"

"Everything is going good."

Me and Denim used condoms each time we fucked, and we were careful about that. The last thing I needed was to be pregnant with his baby. He wasn't talking to me right now and ignored my calls, but I knew he would eventually answer the calls and we would make up just like we were. With Yolani doing everything she should have been doing, I should have been satisfied that Denim backed off and I didn't have to end things. Except, I wasn't, and I was upset. Men got to have their cake and eat it too, why couldn't I? Why couldn't I have my wife and Denim at the same time? The doctor wrote stuff down and the nurse took my cup of piss out of the room. What I was doing was smart, right? Being safe was good, right? Me and Denim may have had a future before I married Yolani, but we didn't have one now. We could never be more than just fucking and cuddling.

Mo told me I needed to leave things alone with Denim. She told me that I was fucking with his feelings and it wasn't fair to him. Yeah, I understood her point, but I didn't give a damn. My feelings for this man was back and I wanted him. Then, I wanted my wife too. Yes, I was selfish and wanted both and was messing with their feelings. For once, I was doing what Hazel wanted and was it wrong that I didn't give a damn how either of them felt? I've always done things everyone has asked of me. Bad relationships, my parents, my business and my wife. I've always taken the L's for all of that. For once, I wanted to be the one doing what she wanted with a smile on her face. Mo would always be Mo and tell me that I was wrong, and it was one of the reasons I loved her. Still, that didn't mean that I was going to stop doing what I pleased when it came to my life. The nurse came in with a folder and handed it to the doctor. He looked at the paper and I studied his face. He didn't appear to be shocked or anything, so everything was normal like I knew it would be.

"Hazel, we won't be doing the birth control today because you're currently pregnant." All the air had been sucked out my lungs when he turned around and told me that. His expression didn't seem like he was shocked at all. Too bad I was paying attention to his facial expression instead of his body language. The man was gripping the counter like he found out that he was fucking pregnant.

"What the fuck do you mean I'm pregnant?"

"The pregnancy test we took came back as positive. You're pregnant, Hazel. I don't mean to pry in your business, however, I need to know. Does your wife know?"

With a blank expression, I rolled my eyes at him. "Do you think she fucking knows?" Getting down from the table, I grabbed my purse. My exam wasn't over, and I still needed to stick around to find more out, and I would in due time. Today, I was past pissed, scared and worried and didn't have time to sit here. Denim was who I needed to see, and I needed to see him – now.

"Hazel, come back, we're not done."

"We're done today. I'll make another appointment." With that, I walked out the exam room and then the office with my phone to my ear. Denim's stupid phone kept going to voicemail, and it was pissing me the hell off. "Listen, I need to talk to you, so stop playing these dumb games and answer the phone." After leaving the voicemail, I went to his sneaker store.

One night after fucking the entire night, he had mentioned he had a lot coming up with his store. It was the afternoon, so I knew he wasn't going to be at his condo unless he was taking the day off. Knowing Denim, taking the day off was like a slow torture to him.

His sneaker store was in Harlem, which wasn't too far from where I was at. Pregnant? How could I be fucking pregnant? I was so careful; we were so careful. Even when we fucked, he pulled out. Yes, I knew that method didn't always work, but he had a condom on, so it should have worked. What the fuck was I supposed to do? Was I supposed to act like Yolani's strap on got me pregnant in Miami? How did I show up to my wife with a baby inside my stomach, knowing she didn't have the equipment to get me pregnant? We wiped our slate clean in Miami, so I couldn't bring up old shit to justify the fact that I went out, cheated and came back pregnant. The only person I thought to call was Golden. She had given me her number when I was over at the house a few weeks ago. We sent text messages back and forth, but nothing more. The reason I thought to call her was because she wasn't close to the situation. She didn't know Yolani or Denim. Shit, she barely knew me, so she couldn't judge. Not to mention, she was sleeping in a car not too long ago with a kid, so her room for judgment was out the window.

"Hey Hazel!" her perky voice beamed through the phone.

"Hey Golden, you busy? Is Yoshon near you?"

"Yoshon?" she giggled his name like a silly school girl. Usually, I would pry and try to be nosey and I would eventually. Right now, it was about me and this crisis that I was having.

"Yes, is he around you?"

"Oh, no. I'm actually heading to his tanning salon to interview some potential employees. What's going on?"

"I'm pregnant!" I blurted.

"Um, congrats, right? Pit Pat didn't mention that you both were trying. I'm happy for you and I can't wait to meet Yolani."

"Because we weren't. I'm cheating on Yolani."

"Oh, so this is bad. What are you going to do? Was it a one-night stand? Did you do it on purpose because she wasn't paying you any attention?"

"Golden, stop speaking so fast and asking so many questions. He's my ex and kind of. Denim gave me attention when Yolani wasn't. I got caught up and now I fucked up."

"Let me ask you this, how do you feel?"

"Scared."

"Well, duh. Besides scared. Do you think you can be a mother?"

"I do, but not like this. Yolani would never accept this baby and will divorce me. I can't have his baby; it's out the question."

"Well, it sounds like you made up your choice. Why did you call me?"

"I needed someone who wasn't so close to the situation to vent to."

"Hazel, I don't know much about you and Yolani's situation, and I don't care to know. One thing I do know, this baby isn't a mistake, and it's a blessing. No matter the outcome of your marriage, you need to focus on that child first. I'm not judging if you get an abortion, but get one for the right reasons, not because your wife won't accept it."

What Golden said to me was true. Then, I thought about Yolani's face and my opinion switched. "Thanks, I need to go handle something."

"Okay. Good luck." She ended the call.

Parking in front of his sneaker store was thick, so I double parked. Rushing inside, I found Denim talking to two other men. When he saw me and my face, he knew I was about to start shit. Before he could fully make it over to me, I started talking.

"You can ignore my calls, but be up in here smiling and laughing with these niggas?"

"They're my business partners, so you need to chill. Fuck with my heart, fine. But, when you fuck with my money, I'm not about to tolerate it. Go your ass to my office and wait for me to come."

Just like he said, my ass was walking to his office and I plopped down. I always wanted kids and I had brought it up to Yolani plenty of times. She didn't want children and voiced her opinion about it. She told me that she didn't want a mini her looking up to her and possibly failing them. Her whole look on parenting was warped and I never tried to change it because I knew all she been through. Being a mother is something that I wanted to be, just not like this. It couldn't be like this.

"The fuck was that about?" he came into the office and closed the door behind him. "Don't fuck with my money, Hazel. You'll meet another Denim if you do that shit." He was serious and the vein in his neck was bulging out.

"I'm pregnant." There was no other way that I could say it or soften the blow. At this point, it was what it was.

His expression softened. "Seriously?"

"Yes. I literally came straight from the doctor's office."

"You keeping it?"

"No." My lips moved without me thinking. My brain had already made up a decision and it was one I needed to roll with. Bringing a baby into this mess wasn't going to be smart.

"What the fuck you mean, no?"

"How do you really think I can come and tell Yolani that I'm pregnant? I'm not going to deliver a plastic baby, Denim."

"Look, I don't give a fuck about her. I care about my child you're carrying. Why the fuck do you think you can make decisions like it won't affect me?"

"It's my body, Dem. Things are going right in my marriage and I can't chance this." He leaned on the wall and chuckled like I had just said the most funniest shit he had heard.

"What the hell is so funny?"

"How you running around claiming that you're her wife, and you're not even legally married?" he continued to laugh.

"Yes, we are. I was fucking there and we got married." The day we got married, it was small, and we had one of Yoshon's judge friends do the wedding. He married us, and Yolani told me she got the papers from him and all I needed to do was to sign, and everything would be done.

"Nah, you filed for a marriage license, but the shit was never filed. You're not legally married, and I looked that shit up." He went behind his desk and pulled some papers out and handed it to me.

Right in my face, staring me was our information and Yoshon's friend never filed the certificate after he married us. This entire time I thought I was married and I wasn't legally married. Did Yolani know about this? Was this the reason that my name wasn't on the house or any of her bank accounts. Or why she kept putting off opening our joint account?

"W...why did you look this up?"

"You're fucking life is a lie, but you so busy trying to run from the one thing true in your life, Hazel. Ask wifey why she never had the documents filed. I'm sure she knows all about it."

"Fuck you, Denim!" I screamed and left his office and store. Today was a day that I would never forget. If I chose to have this baby, I would tell him all about the day I found out about him. He came and stirred chaos into my life today. Getting into the car, I headed straight home. All the way home, I did eighty to ninety miles on the freeway. I needed to get home; I just needed to reach there quick.

You could tell something was wrong from the way I pulled into the driveway. Yoshon's car was in the driveway. Great, this is just what the fuck I needed. When I walked through the door, I could smell pine sol and bleach. Pit Pat was doing her last bit of cleaning before she headed back home. It was nice having her here, not for the cooking or cleaning. Having someone to come home to was nice for a change. Usually, I came home to an empty house, and it got lonely at times.

"What's good, Hazel?" Yoshon nodded as he ate a sandwich.

"Hey," my reply was dry and I knew it was. His would be dry too if he found out all that I found out.

"Hazel, come upstairs, I need to show you something in your closet."

"Ready for her to come home, nasty?"

"What you talking about?"

"One word; Golden," was all I said and headed upstairs. This nigga stood there with a silly grin on his face.

When I got upstairs, Pit Pat was waiting in my bedroom. "Hazel, I don't want to say this in front of Yoshon. He doesn't need to know this," she started. I could see the worry in her face from how she was speaking to me.

"Pit Pat, what's wrong?"

"I don't get into y'alls business, but Yolani a damn crack head," she whispered to me. "I found this in her jeans while doing laundry."

"Pit, you know she works around that stuff too."

"It was empty, Hazel. I know my granddaughter, and she hasn't been herself lately, and I knew something was up, I just didn't know it was this bad." Tears fell down her cheeks.

"I wouldn't worry about it. She works around it and probably had it in her pocket or something." Here I was downplaying it and Pit Pat took it upon herself.

"This is downplaying it, Hazel? She has a box under her side of the bed with empty baggies. They're used." She showed me the box and reality hit me. Here I thought Yolani was cheating on me and she was actually using coke. As if today couldn't get any worse. Plopping on the bed, I put my head in my hands. Was this my karma for cheating on my fake marriage? Lord, please give me a sign because I was completely lost and confused on what step I should make next.

18

Yoshon

"MA, YOU GOTTA GET UP," I kissed Golden on the cheek to wake her. She groaned and pushed me away. "Gyan about to get up and he can't see you leaving my room. Your rule, remember? I mean, if you want him to know, I don't have no problem with it."

"No, no, no, I'm not even sure what we're doing so I'm not about to confuse him." She sat up in the bed.

"I know what we're doing and what we've been doing," I smirked and she hit me.

"Pit Pat doesn't even know about us, and she's about to get up in a bit." She pulled the covers off her body and slipped her feet into her slippers.

"They all could know about us."

"No, Yoshon. You promised me," she brought up the bullshit promise I made her.

After we spent the night fucking, she made me promise that I wouldn't involve my family and she wouldn't involve Gyan. What we were doing would stay between the both of us until we both said otherwise. How does she expect me to agree to something like that when I just climbed out some good ass pussy? Golden had me ready to call Grape and tell him that I found the one. This feeling I felt around her, it had been a while since I had felt that way about someone. She made me laugh, and I don't mean a regular laugh. Shorty had me laughing all goofy in front of her. I made it home every night, but she had me coming home earlier because I couldn't wait to sit across from her and Gyan while eating dinner. Pussy was just an added bonus to all of it.

"Ight, I promised. Give me a kiss and get out my room."

She bent down and kissed me. "Don't be shady now. Get some sleep because you need to head to the city today."

"Yeah, I hear you," I mumbled as she left my room quietly, like she did every night. Some nights I would sleep in her room, but after Gyan walked in her room in the middle of the night, she came to my room instead.

Golden was scared and hesitant to move quick, where I was ready to move like yesterday. I had to respect her wishes because she had a son to think about. At the end of the day, what she chose to do had to involve her son, and I respected it. As I laid back down, I stared up at the ceiling and thought about how that fat ass looked when I hit it from the back. The way she moaned my name and then sucked on my bottom lip when she was fucking the shit out of me. Lil' mama was a fucking freak and she liked to play like she didn't know how to fuck the soul out of a nigga. Golden wanted to keep shit quiet between us and I was going along with it. Knowing Pit Pat, she was going to figure shit out way before we decided to tell them. She didn't miss anything and wouldn't hesitate to tell us that she knew. The plus was that she actually liked Golden and Gyan.

Looking at my clock, it was five in the morning. After

spending last night together, my ass wasn't going back to sleep. Sitting up in the bed, I scrolled my missed messages and sighed when I saw Eva's name with seven messages attached to it. I told her I needed time and it was true, I did. She was getting too fucking clingy and assuming shit that I told her would never be. The way she showed her ass when Golden let her in the crib, I knew I needed to step back from her. Grape's number had stood out to me.

Yo, we coming through for some of Pit Pat's breakfast in the morning. Fear is in town.

Word? Come through.

Me and my nigga, Fear went way back. That nigga and me broke so much bread together that we were both rich. If I would have known he was coming into town, I would have arranged for him to come stay with me at the crib. This nigga was the most loyal nigga I knew. Last we spoke, he was trying to find a wife and settle the fuck down. I told his ass he needed to move to New York and get him a chick. It wasn't nothing like a woman from New York. Yeah, they gave headaches because they take shit, but in the end, you knew you had a real and trill ass woman.

Sayless. I checked my phone and then turned over, so I could get some sleep. When I heard Pit Pat's slippers slide across the floors, I knew she was about to make breakfast for a damn army. Since my grandmother been back home, something had been on her mind. I couldn't place my finger on it, but she was going through something and didn't want to talk about it. Me and Yolani had been like two ships in the night and kept missing each other. It had been a minute since she came through and we had a talk. It was long due, and I made sure to make a mental note to speak to her about it later on today.

I slept for a good three hours before Grape called me and told me they were on their way. I showered and got ready for the day. After having lunch with them, I knew I had to check on a few things. Golden was still doing interviews at the tanning salon, so she would be busy with that for the day. As I came downstairs, Pit Pat was already talking and laughing with Gyan. Their morning routine consisted of corny *knock knock* jokes and other jokes they could find on the internet. I was about to join in on their corny morning jokes when the doorbell rang. I went to the door and Grape, and Fear was standing there.

"My niggaaaaa," I dapped him and pulled him into a brotherly hug.

"Look at this place... nigga living large. Selling all those damn guns got you living like this? Shit, I may need to switch businesses," he joked and dapped me back.

"I try, I try. Can't live in the hood forever, right?"

"Not at all, but we can buy it up, flip it and make the hood better. Gotta give back to what raised us, feel me?"

"I hear you, I hear you," I laughed and showed them into the kitchen. "Pit Pat, Grape and Fear is going to be joining us for breakfast."

She had her back turned making the eggs. "It's more than enough to go around. I know your friend got a damn name... I deal with Grape's nickname, but Fear, I need a real name."

"Grand!" I heard Golden's voice from behind me.

Gyan turned around in his seat. "Dad?"

TO BE CONTINUED

Should Golden give Yoshon a chance? Was Golden wrong for lying to Yoshon about her past? Is Hazel wrong for playing with Denim's feelings? Should Hazel give Yolani another chance because she's trying to be better as a wife? Should Hazel get rid of her baby, or should she keep her baby?

www.facebook.com/JahquelJ
http://www.instagram.com/_Jahquel
http://www.twitter.com/Author_Jahquel
Be sure to join my reader's group on Facebook
www.facebook.com/ Jahquel's we reading or nah?

Bless Us With A Like!

COMING 05/13!

COMING 05/14!

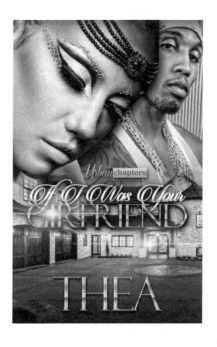